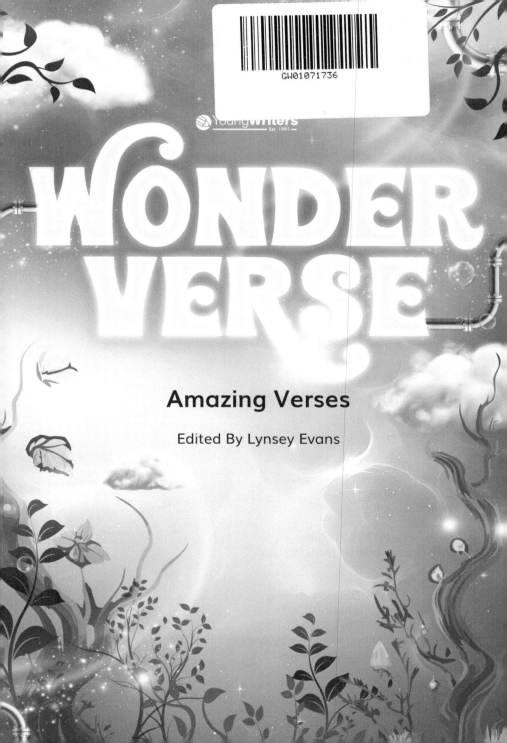

Young**Writers**
— Est. 1991 —

WONDER VERSE

Amazing Verses

Edited By Lynsey Evans

First published in Great Britain in 2025 by:

Young Writers
Remus House
Coltsfoot Drive
Peterborough
PE2 9BF
Telephone: 01733 890066
Website: www.youngwriters.co.uk

FOREWORD

WELCOME READER,

For Young Writers' latest competition *Wonderverse*, we asked primary school pupils to explore their creativity and write a poem on any topic that inspired them. They rose to the challenge magnificently with some going even further and writing stories too! The result is this fantastic collection of writing in a variety of styles.

Here at Young Writers our aim is to encourage creativity in children and to inspire a love of the written word, so it's great to get such an amazing response, with some absolutely fantastic pieces. This open theme of this competition allowed them to write freely about something they are interested in, which we know helps to engage kids and get them writing. Within these pages you'll find a variety of topics, from hopes, fears and dreams, to favourite things and worlds of imagination. The result is a collection of brilliant writing that showcases the creativity and writing ability of the next generation.

I'd like to congratulate all the young writers in this anthology, I hope this inspires them to continue with their creative writing.

CONTENTS

Saffron Neville (9)	66	Hayley Cartwright (10)	110
Alfie S (9)	67	Sophie Bogdan (10)	111
Anna L (9)	68	Stella Chapman (8)	112
Theodore B (9)	69	Adnae Bateman (10)	113
Sophie Daynes (9)	70	Archie Sandford (9)	114
Millie Poulter (9)	71	Archie Hume (10)	115
David Risk (9)	72	Jasmine Whitehead (8)	116
		Luna Kellitt (10)	117

Penketh South Community Primary School, Penketh

		Izzy Hart (9)	118
		Valentina Guest (8)	119
		Sadie Luck (9)	120
Alex Riley (10)	73	Callum Atherage (10)	121
Emily Massey (10)	74	Harvey Clark (10)	122
Devon McCann (10)	76	Layla Bosworth (9)	123
Eric Sorvel (9)	77	Isla Powell (10)	124
Maicie Roberts (10)	78	Neevie Burfitt-Delord (10)	125
Eva Thomas (9)	79	Annabelle Hadland (9)	126
Isaac Tarbuck (9)	80	Rowan Casey (10)	127
Maya Rolt (9)	81	Ruth Barton (8)	128
William Harris (9)	82	Connie Middleton (11)	129
Aimee-Leigh Brown (9)	83	Bonnie Bruce (10)	130
Manuel Tabi Dueme Jensen (9)	84	Magnus Price (9)	131
Olive Paterson (9)	85	Jonah Dewhurst (10)	132
Ella Vaughan (9)	86	Niamh Jackson (10)	133
Alfie Fitzpatrick (10)	87	Elsie Prigg (8)	134
Alfie Delamere (10)	88	Bella Nash (10)	135
Sophia Prosser (9)	89	Badar Suleman (9)	136
Lacey Pickering (9)	90	Sebby Iordache (9)	137
James Hemsley (9)	91	Frances Boakes (10)	138
		Dilys Fox (10)	139
		Kian Hodgson (10)	140

Red Hill CofE Primary School, Worcester

		Ashton Swindlehurst (8)	141
		Mylan Le (9)	142
Eleanor Lloyd (10)	92	Daisy Carpenter (8)	143
Mabel Ferguson (10)	94	Jess Gunundu (10)	144
Andreas Mougis (11)	96	Willow Rose Forrest (9)	145
Emilia Myers (11)	98	Evelyn Thompson (10)	146
Orla Margetts (10)	100	Poppy Satchwell (10)	147
Joseph Wickson (8)	102	Lochlan O'Loughlin (8)	148
Alanna Lord (10)	103	Edie Worth (11)	149
Farhan Amin (10)	104	Elliott Usher (10)	150
Izaan Ali (9)	106	Amelia Ishaq (10)	151
Noah Keatley (10)	107	Eva Bromage (9)	152
Jude Hulme (10)	108		

Jemima Bartley-Smith (9)	153	Elouise Murphy (10)	196
Charlotte Kenney (11)	154	Isaac Ali (9)	197
Ivy-May Halliday (9)	155	Darcey Ball (9)	198
Matipa Sabaya (9)	156	Isabelle Ford (8)	199
Joseph Cuckston (9)	157	Nancy Mills (9)	200
Mohammed Baruwa (8)	158	Zeke Hodgson (8)	201
Tobias Wung Hean Ko-Newitt (9)	159	Josie Hawkesford (9)	202
Thijs Molenschot (10)	160	Erick Novo (9)	203
Grayson Needs (8)	161	Corey Green (9)	204
Ajwa Ayub (8)	162	Connie Warnett (9)	205
Scarlett Carroll (10)	163	Alanna Taylor (9)	206
George Wiltshire (9) & Henry	164	Scarlett Kidd (9)	207
Bella Jenkins (9)	165	Lucas Sudabby (9)	208
Lucas Burt (9)	166	Arvin Jahani (8)	209
Millie Burt (11)	167	Sidney Thorpe (9)	210
Ben Prigg (9)	168	Mitch Ballinger (9)	211
Charlie-James Humphries (10)	169	Skye Waldron (8)	212
Molly Jane Weaver (9)	170	Layla Al-Najjar (7)	213
Zachary Smith (9)	171	Aaryan Mitchell-Baig (7)	214
Phoebe Dyson-West (10)	172	Ethan Hart (7)	215
Archie Ross (9)	173	Hywel Brown (7)	216
Phoebe Leighton (9)	174	Tiwatope Olabamiyo (7)	217
Jack Kimbell (8)	175	Isla Smith (10)	218
Verity Don Gentry (8)	176	Joshua Evans (10)	219
Teddy Thompson (9)	177	Astrid Bantock-Minton (7)	220
Ella-Rose Crack (9)	178	Eva Arun (7)	221
Alfie Cutler (9)	179	Evyn Schimmel (7)	222
Scarlett Clark (9)	180	Ugochukwu David Anikwe (8)	223
Alfred Cantin (9)	181	Eleanor Foster (7)	224
Sam Bartlett (8)	182	Susie Ross (8)	225
Seb Whelan-Jones (8)	183	Daniel Potter (7)	226
Dulcie Stayte (9)	184	Phoebe Hughes (7)	227
Zoya Riaz (7)	185	Charlie Beddows (10)	228
Ellis Wade (9)	186	Marley Joy Price (7)	229
Holly Scorer (10)	187	Jayden Gardner (9)	230
Martha Casey (9)	188	Sam Hadland (7)	231
Elliott Carroll (8)	189	Myla Holliday (7)	232
Alfie Majhu (8)	190	Atousa Naderasli (7)	233
Oscar McAree (8)	191	Edward Hill (7)	234
Steev Sony (9)	192	Inaaya Shazad (7)	235
Hamza Ali (9)	193	Sam Heydon-Boland (9)	236
Penny Ferguson (7)	194	Rayna Samuel (8)	237
Jack Downing (9)	195	Carys Smith (7)	238

THE CREATIVE WRITING

The Beauty In The Seasons

Winter's gone
Out comes Mrs Swan
Plants are growing
And it's no longer snowing

The sun blazes in different places
Plants, trees and much more grow
And it's not cold, like when there's snow
It's time for fun in the sun

In autumn, the leaves fall one by one
Soon all of them will be gone
Yellow, orange, brown and green
A lot of autumn colours can be seen

The cars turn into snowy, frosted cakes
Covered in little snowflakes
Get wrapped up in your scarves and gloves
And share your holiday with your loves
Get gifts and watch the new year come
Play games with your family, and have a lot of fun.

La'Ren Pennant (9)
Mellers Primary School, Radford

Winter's Arrival

Winter comes and people's thumbs go blue like the snow outside,
I get biscuits, hot chocolate and marshmallows, I sit down and gaze outside
I gaze at the snow falling from the white, fluffy clouds.
I lie down and dream and dream and dream.
I dream about the snow growing high
Up to my knees or up to my height
I wake up and lie there in my bed
Thinking about the day that I had.
As I get out of bed, I put my slippers on my feet
Then walk downstairs to find something to eat.
I look in the fridge to get the ice-cold milk
I look in the cupboard to get something else.
When I've finished my ice-cold milk
I go upstairs to watch the snow.

Hafsah Shaw (9)
Mellers Primary School, Radford

The Life Rhyme

On a sunny day
The birds tweet
I am in my room, listening to the beat
I hear pancakes flipping in a pan
I am outside, having a tan
Nutella on pancakes, with honey too.
Wembley Stadium is saying, "Boo!"
We go to school at 8:40
I wish on Fridays there were parties
In school, there are playtime and loos
We learn science, geography and maths too
We have to be generous and have pride
We go to the sea and see a big tide.
This is the end of this rhyme.
Hope you had a good time.
See you again another time.

Ali Idris (9)
Mellers Primary School, Radford

Dream On, Samuel

In a small village lived young Samuel,
Who had big ambitions in life,
He wore torn-up shoes and boots,
He had a heart so bold in a world of grey,

His family's table often lacked food,
Yet his eyes glimmered despite the despair,
He envisioned MUGAs where he would run and play,
A football merchant no matter the challenges,

Each day, after school, he envisioned the game,
Day after day, he would master the game,
Through laughter and tears he made his way,
A boy with dreams that won't be outdone.

Moayed Sharif (9)
Mellers Primary School, Radford

The Dark Den

In the dark, dark den
There's always a creepy man in the window

In the dark, dark den
There are lots of black stains on the house
You go past it, you get the shivers
That's why no one opens the past
People say that the person in the window is a puppet
And some people say that it was a man that got
stuffed and died

In the dark, dark den,
It's very creepy
In the dark, dark den
Which no one likes.

Praise Morris (9)
Mellers Primary School, Radford

Train Ride

You want the green
In your dreams
Get clean, jump on a train
Because it's about to rain
So speak to Jane on the train
You're such a pain
You're on the lane
So have a candy cane
And grow a mane
Whilst I'm in chains
Because I've been a pain
Whilst working on the crane
My blood is being drained
Whilst in the rain
I'm going to drain
You and you're gonna feel pain.

Zidan Salid (9)
Mellers Primary School, Radford

Boom! Crash! Lightning Flash!

Dark clouds gathering
Wind howling
The lightning blasts from the sky
As thunder lashes down in the hectic storm
The treacherous storm turns off all the lights
Whistling wind gnashing its sharp teeth, heard wide
Thunder crashes
Lightning flashes
Heart beating
Wind scattering
The lightning blasts from the sky
Boom! Crash! Lightning flash!

Amina Habbes (9)
Mellers Primary School, Radford

Autumn Season

Leaves go red, orange and gold
I crunch through fallen leaves
The smell of bonfires in the distance
Smoke curls up into the sky

Conkers fall from their spiky shells
And the leaves start to fall from the trees
Pumpkins appear, faces carved into them
Autumn feels like magic all around.

Yasmin Madhat (9)
Mellers Primary School, Radford

Friendship Is A Power

Friends are needed
Friends are kind
Friends are something
You need to have,
To see in the darkness and
It is a power
Friendship is power
Friendship is might
Join the group
And the friendship
So, come on
Be a friend
And you will see
A merry end.

Opeyemi Ogunmadeko (9)
Mellers Primary School, Radford

Robert's Journey To Space

Space vast, empty space
Space is a vast place
A big, gigantic place
Space is empty
Space is vast
Just like Robert's heart
Space is dark and black
Just like Robert's heart
Space, space, space
Robert wants to go to space.

Excellent (9)

Mellers Primary School, Radford

Heartfire

D ragons create fire from,
R ays of the sun,
A lthough they have the ability to breathe fire,
G etting their inner heartfire lets them create fire,
O n the most freezing,
N ights of this mystical, magical world.

Ayaan Farooque (9)
Mellers Primary School, Radford

Winter And Summer

Winter's here and so am I
I like snow and you like sunshine
I like hot chocolate and you like lemonade
I like chocolate and you like sweets
I like Christmas and you like the seaside
I like the winter and you like the summer.

Rajveer Maya Kaur (10)
Mellers Primary School, Radford

The Dark Serpent

Deep in the ocean, where the dark creatures lay,
Far, far, far away, where monsters go to stay,
Above the waters, where the chaos sways,
The luck of the sea, where everyone gets saved.

In the distance, where no island shall be,
Stormy weather, where it disappears into the sea,
The horrid hurricane, that makes whirlpools,
With the tail, like lightning, crushing the walls.

The moon is as white as a balloon.
Back on land, where the blossom trees bloom,
Venom as black as tar,
Many battles where I have scars.

When you travel on the seas,
Make sure you don't get caught by the gleaming beams,
On the bottom of the ocean floor,
Where the different types of coral lay, as before.

Phoebie Warner (8)
Newport Primary School, Newport

Happiness

Happiness is a vibrant yellow, like pollen from a flower,
Happiness is glistening grass after a gentle morning
shower.

Happiness is the taste of a freshly baked cupcake,
Happiness is real, it can never be fake.

Happiness is the smell of a chocolate bar, unwrapped,
Happiness is the cutest puppy who yaps, and yaps, and
yaps.

Happiness is the shape of a beaming love heart,
Happiness is when people compliment your art.

Happiness is the sound of children laughing non-stop,
Happiness is when you get something from your
favourite shop.

Happiness is the feeling of snuggling under a duvet,
Happiness is when your friend comes over to play.

Sienna (9)
Newport Primary School, Newport

Joy

Joy is like a slice of heaven,
Even luckier than the number seven.

It smells like pizza, served on a golden plate,
It's like hanging out with your favourite mate.

It feels like you're on top of the world,
It was as if sadness had been hurled.

It looks like a ray of that comforting sun,
It's like playing sports, which to me is quite fun.

It sounds like children playing in the streets,
It's like slipping into those warm, clean sheets.

It tastes like a glorious victory,
It's like working in your favourite factory.

Joy is where you just feel elated,
It will always, always make you feel exhilarated.

Henry Frier (10)
Newport Primary School, Newport

Fear

Fear is black like a cloudy, night sky, a cloud of pain
that rejects to leave you alone

It tastes like salty water, fresh from the depths of the
sea, like a wave making you drink the water

It smells damp and rotten, like walking into a colossal
bin filled with rotting mouldy food left for weeks

It looks like a world of nightmares, all laid upon a
stormy cloud of torture and regret

It sounds like a booming voice, so loud that it's like it's
using a microphone through speakers that makes it
echo

It feels sad but at the same time scared, like being all
alone, lost whilst not knowing which way home or
where to go.

Theo Pereira (9)
Newport Primary School, Newport

Sadness

Sadness is blue, like a tear rolling down a cheek,
It's as if your eyes were always going to leak.

It tastes like the lonely egg, the last in the box,
It's like joy is kept away inside its locks.

It looks like rain hitting a puddle,
And like your mother won't give you a cuddle.

It sounds like crying from the room next door,
It's so sad like it's burning through your core.

It smells like impending doom, hanging in the air,
When you're sad, you don't think anything is fair.

Sadness feels like a devastating day,
You feel crestfallen, is what I would say.

Gianluca Stabellini (9)
Newport Primary School, Newport

Sadness

Sadness is blue like the wet, pouring rain on a cold
winter's day
It's like you're being asked if you're okay

It tastes like salty sea water washed up ashore
It roots you deep into the core

It smells like a lonely, snowy Christmas night
While all the lanterns are lit with light

It looks like a smashed bowl on the hard floor
Like your heart couldn't take anymore

It sounds like a gentle sobbing in a corner
Soon your tears cause your cheeks to swell up and get
warmer

It feels like you're swiping your hand through running
water
It makes you even feel shorter.

Neave F (9)
Newport Primary School, Newport

The Deadly Forest

The bright orange fox strolled across the wet green
grass as if he were the king of the forest
His orange tail swishing like leaves on a branch
His jagged teeth snapping like an angry crocodile
His eyes glowing like two orange lanterns in the night

The tiny rabbit gazed at his jagged teeth as if he were
a midnight feast
His miniature ears fell down like a dead flower when he
saw his pointed yellow teeth

The statuesque tree stood silently like a frozen flame,
an owl inside the hole of shame
The black leaves slowly fall off the rotten old tree like
autumn days
Mould on the tree like a frozen pond.

Martha Sloan (8)
Newport Primary School, Newport

The Deadly Serpent

The ravishing moon and stars are like elegant balloons.
Its sharp teeth are like shards of glass.
It is going to put a hole in your galleon and will make it sink.
Bloodshot eyes so bright, you can see them in the fog,
With bijou but beady pupils.
Black venom shoots from its fangs, leaving a trail wherever it goes.
It can demolish anything it wants with a splash.
Its flawless tail is a whip of the sea.
The calm sea hates the serpent because it incessantly splashes its smooth surface.
Teeth, like colossal walls of swords, snap at its prey.
If you see it, sail away!

Bella Knight (9)
Newport Primary School, Newport

The Deadly Serpent

The body is shiny, scaly, spiky,
The sharp teeth are venomous, too,
Its bloodshot eyes are like X-rays scanning the horizon,
The scales shine like diamonds in the sky,
In the dead of night, the teeth are fluorescent,
The sun is shining and the serpent is sleeping.

Its tail is as sharp as a knife,
The body is as long as a galleon,
In the pitch-black night, its demon eyes are deadly.

Beware the incessant hissing,
Like wind in a vacant canyon,
When it is morning, the serpent is snoring,
When it is night, the eyes are bright.

Olivia Lindsay (8)
Newport Primary School, Newport

The Sparkly Sea Serpent

The bright moon shines on the water,
The blue, sparkling waves crash rapidly
Against the serpent's slimy body.
The scaly, blue serpent swooshes through the
glimmering water,
Like a snake slithering in the sand.

Its long, rough tail splashes solidly,
Its gleaming, red eyes are always watching,
Like a hawk following its prey.
Razor-sharp, enormous teeth, always ready to strike.

It quickly glides through the water as it hunts,
It sees the glamorous galleon sailing through the
ocean,
It skims across the water, and strikes.

Esme Stevens (8)
Newport Primary School, Newport

Anger

Anger is red, like a ball of flames
It starts with embarrassment, or maybe shame

It tastes like a stale piece of cake in a box
And it's always alone, like an angry fox

It smells like a burning piece of toast
Or maybe a smelly Sunday roast

It looks like torture from the Devil
Trying to keep cool and keep my head level

It sounds like the screams inside my head
Feeling like I'm almost dead

It feels like a stab, deep in my heart
I am lost and don't know where to start.

Jude Smith (9)
Newport Primary School, Newport

Slithering Serpent

The bright moon shines on the water
The blue, sparkling waves crash rapidly
Against the serpent's slimy body
The scaly, blue serpent swooshes
The glimmering water, like a snake in the sand
Its long, rough tail splashes solidly into the water
Its gleaming, red eyes are always watching
Like a hawk following its prey
Razor-sharp, enormous teeth, always ready to strike
It quickly glides through the water as it hunts
It sees the glamorous galleon sailing through the ocean
It skims across the water, and strikes!

Joseph (8)
Newport Primary School, Newport

Joy

Joy is like a dazzling yellow,
Joy will make you sound mellow.

Joy tastes like fresh marshmallows out of the bag,
Like in your parent's favourite mag.

Joy smells like your home,
Joy also smells like pine needles and pinecones.

Joy is like the cutest dog,
Joy will make you want to read whilst sitting on a log.

Joy sounds like happy children talking,
Joy is when you're skipping and walking.

Joy feels like a soft teddy bear,
Joy is when people say they really care!

Harriet Bell (9)
Newport Primary School, Newport

Anger

Anger is red, like a fire set in a town,
Then the ashes will melt to the ground.
It tastes like hot pepper filled with smoke.
In a dark room, with not a single joke.
It smells the opposite of a marshmallow,
But it can be rude to an old fellow.
It looks like you just got fired from your job,
And you wanted to get revenge on your boss, Bob.
It sounds like you are shouting loudly at your enemy for
two hours,
While you are at Disney, Paris, on the highest tower.
It feels like your friends have left you alone.

June (9)
Newport Primary School, Newport

The Deadly Beast!

As the moon shimmers in the night,
Out of the shadows comes a terrifying sea serpent.
Its bloodshot eyes are like balls of fire,
Its teeth are small, rusty bits of metal,
And when you hear a sudden growl,
You know to run and flee!

Its tail is like a knife,
Slicing through anything that gets in its way.
It destroys so many galleons,
You can see its tail is covered in splinters and cuts!
This creature is slyer than a fox,
Quicker than a tidal wave,
So, beware of the deadly sea beast!

Bethany (8)
Newport Primary School, Newport

Fear

Fear is black as the darkest night
There is no way being led to light

Its only taste is dark and miserable
The thought of death is inconsiderable

It smells like nothing but dead trees
I don't think I am asking with a please

Fear looks like a lonely cow in a field
It is behind its mighty shield

It sounds like the deafening of an ear
And a lonely person cuddling in fear

Fear feels like a sad cold
I don't think anyone would want to be in this mess.

Maurice Green (9)
Newport Primary School, Newport

Deadly Serpent

The moon is as giant as a balloon as it appears.
It makes an attractive incessant hiss.
His elegant eyes gleam like lanterns on the sea as they
gaze at people.
His giant spikes are pointing like a pin in the water.
Its exquisite body is a river of muscle.
It's got sparkling scales like the moon.
Its tail whips through the calm waves, making rough
seas.
Venom as black as tar.
Out of the shadows.
Scales shimmering like coins in the moonlight.
Beware of this deadly serpent.

Ferne Bayford (8)
Newport Primary School, Newport

Sly Serpent

Its beady eyes are like mini lanterns peering out to sea,
looking for prey,
It's always out at night but never in the day,
Its charming tail is whipping the sea hundreds of miles
away from where the serpent lies,
Sometimes, it roars so loud that sailors hear children's
cries,

It roars at the full moon like it's hoping to scare the
moon and cause a pitch-black night,
Its body is so long and scary, it will cause quite a fright,
This deadly, sly serpent is a tidal wave.

Anabelle (8)
Newport Primary School, Newport

Fire-Breathing Serpent

Its fire-breathing mouth is like a tempestuous storm
Its vacant face makes it look incessantly angry
Its flawless screech echoes as it travels through an
indulgent cave over the vast ocean
Its deadly eyes are bloodshot like a glowing red pen
Its teeth demolish everything it eats
Its spiky back slithers onto the solid water
Its tail is menacing like a whip smacking the water
which is as hard as rock
The sea is a blue marshmallow carrying this enormous
fire-breathing serpent.

Evie Mardell (8)
Newport Primary School, Newport

Deadly Serpent

Its terrifying, bloodshot eyes are unsettling
Its giant spikes like razor-sharp blades
Its body is strong enough to leap up out of the huge,
tempestuous waves like a gigantic spring
Its incessant hiss, horrid,
Its flawless tail is a whip of the sea
Below the tempestuous waves, it waits for the perfect
moment to attack
As if a silent jack-in-a-box
When you see a snake-like shadow under the deep,
dark... *Sail away!*

Conor R (8)
Newport Primary School, Newport

The Poisonous Serpent

The serpent has teeth as sharp
As little daggers.

It can eat whole fish in one
Gulp.

It lives in shipwrecks that are
As large as cargo ships.

The serpent hunts its prey with
Its dark red eyes.

In the night-time, this living
Tidal wave circles ships to sink
Them.

It can travel through seas and
Oceans as quickly as lightning.

Sam Knight (9)
Newport Primary School, Newport

The Deadly Beast!

The crescent moon is as white as a cloud
Out of the shadows lurks a terrifying creature coming
up from the depths of the tempestuous sea
You can see its dark scales shimmer in the light of the
moon

Its eyes are like two red moons on its head
Its teeth are sharp daggers that can bite through
anything
Its tail is a whip smashing against the waves with
sharp spikes on the end.

Joel (8)
Newport Primary School, Newport

The Great Flying Donkey

The flying donkey has strong wings, like an aeroplane.
Its spiky tail is purple, black, and green, shimmering like
a coin.
Its colossal eyes are shining brightly, like burning coal.
Its ears are orange and black, like soft velvet.
With his pristine tail, he can demolish a wooden
galleon with one flick.
Beware of this fluffy, but deadly, mysterious creature.

Arthur Roach (8)

Newport Primary School, Newport

Venomous Superstitious Serpent

Below the sparkling moon, a black African serpent lurks.
Its teeth are like spinning blades.
Its bloodshot eyes gaze out to sea at its prey.
Its tail is like a sword slicing through.
The colossal scales are deadly arrows.
An incessant siren in the fog
Is a warning of tempestuous waves.
This sea serpent is the most deadly creature in the ocean.

Atalia Salawu (8)
Newport Primary School, Newport

Cunning Serpent

Its beady eyes are like lanterns in the fog,
You can see its teeth are sharp shards of glass,
Its body is like a sly snake, going into the tempestuous ocean.

You can hear the suspicious screeching noises through the wind,
Its body is a tightly coiled spring of muscle, waiting to pounce,
Its dangerous tail snakes against the stormy ocean.

Elsie (8)
Newport Primary School, Newport

Fear

Fear is as black as a gloomy night sky,
Charging through a tranquil forest.

It smells like rotten skin,
That's been touched by death itself.

It tastes like human bone,
Engulfed in flames.

It feels like a snowman,
Lying in the middle of winter.

It looks like depression and isolation.

Oscar Wool (9)
Newport Primary School, Newport

Autumn

A utumn leaves crunch like crisps

U mbrellas pop up like blooming flowers

T rick or treating as a zombie

U nder the ground, animals hibernating like sleeping people.

M uddy leaves lie on the floor like tired people

N ests are built for birds to stay in the winter and autumn.

Ellie Featherstone (7)
Newport Primary School, Newport

Autumn

A mazing, colourful leaves, lie crisp on the ground
U nder a blanket with hot chocolate, like a fire
T urning cold, like a piece of frozen food
U nder the ground, hibernating animals are as warm
    as can be
M uddy wellingtons are splashing in puddles
N ow nights get longer!

Lily (7)
Newport Primary School, Newport

Autumn

A utumn leaves like a red apple

U nderground sleeping flowers like hibernating hedgehogs

T rees are brown like conkers

U mbrellas pop up on a rainy day like us jumping

M uddy marks on a rainy day like footprints in the snow

N ests waiting for birds as we wait for warmth.

Charlotte Frier (7)
Newport Primary School, Newport

The Golden Dragon

A golden dragon like a huge house,
His long legs can easily break the wooden galleon,
His sharp teeth can easily demolish everything.

His eyes are red but not bloodshot,
His tail can splash the water, whipping it up into a tempestuous sea,
His massive neck can stretch up to the grey midnight moon.

George M (8)
Newport Primary School, Newport

The Tall Serpent

The serpent haunts the sea at night
Lurking at the bottom of the cold black ocean
The serpent's teeth are like sharpened daggers
With a strong terrifying bite
The serpent is as long as a skyscraper is tall
Its body is a river of muscle
The serpent's eyes are black like pools of darkness.

Ollie Martin (9)
Newport Primary School, Newport

Anger

Anger is red, like a crackling fire.
It tastes like burnt toast on fire.
It smells like charcoal, burning for a fire.
It looks like a burning house, engulfed in fire.
It sounds like when you throw conkers in a fire.
It feels like you're going to burst into flames, like a bonfire.
Anger is fire.

Hugo Mathias (9)
Newport Primary School, Newport

The Serpent

The serpent haunts the sea at night, lurking at the bottom of the cold, black ocean.
The serpent's teeth are like sharpened daggers, with a strong, terrifying bite.
The serpent is as long as a skyscraper is tall.
Its body is a river of muscle.
The serpent is as heavy as twenty double-decker buses.

Jacob (8)
Newport Primary School, Newport

The Bloodshot Serpent

The serpent is as soft as silk
It lives at the bottom of the Pacific Ocean in a gloomy cave
When the moon is a white balloon, the serpent leaves his lair
He screams like a feral wolf and his teeth are as sharp as a steak knife
If you see bloodshot eyes like lanterns lurking in the fog
Beware!

Alex Hyland-Hawkins (8)
Newport Primary School, Newport

Bloodshot Serpent

The serpent haunts the ocean at night.
The serpent's teeth are like small, sharp daggers.
The serpent's bite is as strong as a V8 engine.
The serpent is as long as a skyscraper is tall
Its mouth is a gaping cave.
Its body is a river of muscle.
Its eyes are as big as a globe.

Harvey (8)
Newport Primary School, Newport

Autumn

A utumn leaves are like crisps crunching in our mouths
U mbrellas pop up like flowers
T iny birds grow like flowers blooming
U nder the ground, sleeping flowers like bumblebees
M ilk is hot like hot chocolate
N o sun comes out like flowers.

Amelia (7)
Newport Primary School, Newport

Autumn Days

A brown conker, like hot chocolate burning
U mbrellas popping up, like flowers in spring
T unnelling badgers, like our covers over us
U sual days getting colder
M uddy pigs are running to their houses
N uts are falling off of the trees.

Logan Eameleah Hull (7)
Newport Primary School, Newport

Autumn

A utumn leaves crunch like crisps.
U nder the ground, hedgehogs and badgers hibernating.
T ombolas spinning like the Earth.
U nder the ground, sleeping flowers like animals.
M ake a leaf, craft and play.
N ests waiting for birds.

Isabella Debnam (7)
Newport Primary School, Newport

Frightening Serpent

His scales are as tough as iron.
The serpent is as long as 40,000 buses.
It is as strong as a T-rex's jaw.
It eats every second with its teeth as sharp as arrows.
Its screech is a piercing sound.
Its back is as deadly as a giant wave with electric eels inside.

Noah Travers (8)
Newport Primary School, Newport

Sadness

Sadness, blue like running rain on a dull day
It tastes like sadness, depression, old carrots
It smells like mouldy, expired fruit
It looks like my heart when my ex dumped me
It sounds emotional and sad with vast tears
It feels bad like a naughty girl, all alone.

Sophie Wellington (9)
Newport Primary School, Newport

Anger Is A Devil Shade Of Red

When you make him angry, you're so so done
He feels like an offensive old man exploding with rage.
He smells like freshly burnt charcoal
He's disgusted with himself.
He is an offensive old cruel man
He looks like a red demon being engulfed in fire.

Thomas Woods (9)
Newport Primary School, Newport

Autumn

A utumn leaves crunching like crisps.
U nderground, sleeping flowers.
T rees' leaves falling like parachutes.
U mbrellas popping up like frogs.
M ountains getting cold like ice cubes.
N ests waiting for mother birds.

Alistair Long (7)
Newport Primary School, Newport

Autumn

A utumn approaches, it gets colder and colder
U nder the ground, there are sleeping worms
T rick or treat, like candy and fun
U p in the sky, clouds and clouds
M orning air is cold
N ests have birds sleeping.

George Lewis (7)
Newport Primary School, Newport

Joy

Joy is like a sunflower blooming your day
Can smell like you've found a gold bar
You can overjoy the whole world with joy
If you feel sad it's like a rainy day
Until joy steps in and your rainy day is now a clear blue
sky with a bright sun.

Ted (10)
Newport Primary School, Newport

Autumn

A utumn leaves crunching on the floor
U nder the ground, flowers sleeping like hibernating foxes
T rees losing leaves
U nder the mud worms
M uddy footprints in the house
N est waiting for birds in trees.

Alana Goodyear (8)
Newport Primary School, Newport

Joy

Joy is yellow like a blinding sunset
It tastes like the first slice of candyfloss-flavoured cake
It smells like the open ocean
It looks like the smooth wet sand
It feels like getting a new breathtaking kitten
Joy is found deep in the soul.

Amelia C (9)
Newport Primary School, Newport

Autumn

A utumn days get colder and colder.
U nder the ground, sleeping flowers.
T he nights get darker.
U nder the ground, animals hibernating.
M uddy soil and squelchy mud.
N ight sky is really dark.

Henry Bell (7)
Newport Primary School, Newport

Anger

Anger is red like a burning marshmallow
It tastes like burnt toast
It smells like smoke from a fire
It looks like a laser shining at me
It sounds like paper crackling
It feels like I'm going to explode into monstrous flames.

Harley Reed (9)
Newport Primary School, Newport

The Deadly Serpent

His sharp teeth are like deadly swords
His muscly tail is a lethal weapon
Venom spurts out like spitting poison
His teeth are like shards of glass
Hidden in his colossal mouth
He slithers smoothly and doesn't make a sound.

Alexander S (8)
Newport Primary School, Newport

Joy

Joy is yellow like the beating sun
Joy tastes like ice cream on a warm summer's day
Joy smells like the chlorine from a swimming pool
Joy looks like a field of flowers
Joy sounds like the Easter Bunny laying eggs all
around.

Noah Powell (9)
Newport Primary School, Newport

Sadness

It gives you a shock to your core
It looks like the darkness in a pitch-black room
It sounds like impending doom
It feels like ice-cold water
It tastes like a black void
It smells like tears dripping from your cheek.

TJ (9)
Newport Primary School, Newport

Disgust

Disgust is green like broccoli
She tastes like a mouth full of sick
She smells like sweaty feet
She looks like an autumn leaf
She sounds like she's going to be sick
Disgust feels like a group of sweaty feet.

Mary Long (9)
Newport Primary School, Newport

Autumn

A utumn is cold like an ice cube
U nder the mud, worms live
T rees losing leaves
U nder the ground, sleeping flowers
M isty morning air
N ests waiting for birds in trees.

Ralph Saggers (7)
Newport Primary School, Newport

Joy

Joy is yellow like a tropical bird
It looks like the golden sun
She smells like perfect perfume
She sounds like a beautiful lady
She looks like a glamorous galaxy
She feels like a soft, comforting pillow.

Saffron Neville (9)
Newport Primary School, Newport

Anger

Anger is red like a wild fox
It tastes like a spicy hot pepper
It smells like a puddle of smelly seaweed
It looks like a big fireball
It sounds like an eerie thunderstorm
It feels like a crawling drag.

Alfie S (9)
Newport Primary School, Newport

Joy

Joy is yellow like the sun
It tastes like lemon
It smells like sweets
It looks like the beautiful sun
It sounds like jingle bells ringing on Santa's sleigh
It feels like great happiness.

Anna L (9)
Newport Primary School, Newport

Joy

Joy is golden like the sun
It tastes like pizza for breakfast
It smells like cake at home
It looks like a gold bay in a pile of sweets
It sounds like drinks on a sunny day
It feels amazing.

Theodore B (9)
Newport Primary School, Newport

Fear

Fear is like the colour of midnight black
Fear tastes like a navy purple musty jumper
It smells like a rotten bin
It looks like a shadow of creepiness
It sounds like a person screaming in fear.

Sophie Daynes (9)
Newport Primary School, Newport

Joy

Joy is as yellow as the bright sun,
Joy tastes like a jar of sweets,
Joy smells like the clean, fresh air,
Joy sounds like happiness coming out of its shell,
Joy feels happy.

Millie Poulter (9)
Newport Primary School, Newport

Anger

Anger is red like a firework
And smells like a bonfire
It tastes like a burnt pancake
And looks like a red flame
Anger sounds like a phoenix
And feels angry and livid.

David Risk (9)
Newport Primary School, Newport

New School, New Life, New World!

When I moved house, I felt like a mouse
Scared, alone, as if I was being chased by a cat
Then along came a friend
We made amends
And now we are *best* friends
Her name is Emily, and she is very brave
For she chased the cat away into its cave
So I know I'm safe with her
Safe with her
Safe and sound
She'd stick up for me
Like in PE
When some others had it out for me
Or when I'm alone
Or walking home
She's the one who brightens my day
And takes the darkness away
And all the worries away
Sometimes I'm grumpy and I take it out on her.

Alex Riley (10)
Penketh South Community Primary School, Penketh

Foliage Fables

Look at all these green leaves
Yet golden in the autumn
Look, there's some wood, it must be a tree!
And I'm sure that everybody loves them

Take for instance the alder
Which is a very dark tree
Let's try and help it as much as we can
Because sadly it's at risk of disease

Now see the weeping willow
Oh, why is she always so sad?
Her name is so pretty and so is her appearance
So I think that she should be glad

Oh wow, it's a birch!
It's Snow White if she were a plant
The bark is very thin and the colour of the clouds
So everyone starts to chant

Next, we'll view the oak
Where the forest fairies fly
The acorns, they hang and the squirrels like it too
Mmm... I wonder why.

Have a merry Christmas! Last, it's holly.
Mostly used for festive wreaths
It grows little red berries, though not very tasty
It's one of the only evergreen broadleaves!

Please help our trees, they are dying out
Their numbers are slowly dwindling
Their coverage of the UK is only 13%
So please, please, please help our trees.

Emily Massey (10)
Penketh South Community Primary School, Penketh

Dance Competition Day (Falling In Style)

The towering theatre comes up upon us.
Waiting at the bus stop we chat like monkeys in the zoo.
Getting our perfect passes with our perfect pictures,
Going into the eerie basement dressing room.
Putting on the leopard suit and final touches, adding poms.
Watching from behind the curtain ready to go on, argh!
Looking for when I'm on.
Getting in position, the music starts,
I start to dance and...
I trip and fall flat on my face... OMG!
Luckily I fall into the splits but I'm down, down, down!
But I get up and continue to finish...
And we win!

Devon McCann (10)
Penketh South Community Primary School, Penketh

Teaming Technology

Techno TV, Xbox 360, short programs
In movies advancing came around
Robots, AI, phrasing, crashing,
It's bad for your eyes
Argh internet wires snapping
Expensive Nintendo Switch
More advancing came around
Oh no, PlayStation 5, Pro-E 700
This is too much
It was always fine until it came
Taking over toy shops nonstop
Robs even more
Advancing came around
Absolutely not Disney+, Sky, Netflix, no
Everyone staying inside
Argh, I am... Doh!

Eric Sorvel (9)
Penketh South Community Primary School, Penketh

Panda World

Your crunch of bamboo
The world is now blue
Roses are red
Like your small crazy bed
Show emotion
The world is certain
Your long strong fur
The heart is your cure
The family grew
The world was a shoe
The world was poor
There was no more
The cutdown trees
The world would freeze
The pandas grew
The world was too true
Your black fur
The night blurs
Your big tree
The world was three.

Maicie Roberts (10)
Penketh South Community Primary School, Penketh

The Cat World

Your happy, calm purring
Sounds like the world swirling
The long whiskers
The quiet whispers
Your wiggly tail
My ponytail
Your sharp claws
The world's paw
Bits of white
The big fight
Cats grow
The world grew
Your white fur
The small purr
The world was poor
There was no more
Your mighty claw
Your sharper jaw
The big munch
The tiny punch.

Eva Thomas (9)
Penketh South Community Primary School, Penketh

A Little Something About Monsters

Do you even know if monsters are really bad?
For example...
The werewolf is an artist, not a maneater
The Cyclops plays football
Bigfoot and Yeti play basketball and do not terrorise people
The giant plays rugby, by far the best
The goblins play baseball and
The elves play hockey, the best team by far
You see these monsters are not bad at all
They are just misunderstood.

Isaac Tarbuck (9)
Penketh South Community Primary School, Penketh

Spooky Season Is Here

H orrifying costumes

A rgh!

L isten carefully, or you will get a trick!

L ooking at all my sweets!

O ctober 29th is when it gets exciting.

W atching people go trick or treating.

E xciting.

E veryone going to very scary houses.

N ever going to that house again!

Maya Rolt (9)

Penketh South Community Primary School, Penketh

The Cabin In The Woods

Late one stormy night deep in the spooky forest
There was an old cabin in the woods
One night, however, two kids found this old cabin
They went inside, the door slammed shut
It was locked
They started looking through each room
There was no way out
To this day their souls haunt the cabin in the woods.

William Harris (9)
Penketh South Community Primary School, Penketh

Halloween Time

Red and yellow leaves everywhere
That means it is time for a Halloween fair
Look at the mist in the sky
Think about the pumpkin pie
It is time for the Halloween decorations
Am excited to see the pumpkin-carved creations
I have lots of lovely sweets
People are coming to trick or treat.

Aimee-Leigh Brown (9)
Penketh South Community Primary School, Penketh

Gaming

People click me
And I am controlled by a monitor
And I go on a pad
What am I?

I am the one who controls the whole system
I am shaped like a cube
What am I?

I am a rectangle
And I am used to see what people are doing
What am I?

Manuel Tabi Dueme Jensen (9)
Penketh South Community Primary School, Penketh

Everything At Once

As hot as the sun
As fast as a run
As flat as paper
As mean as a hater
As sneaky as a fox
As strong as an ox
As cold as ice
As slimy as slime
As straight as a line
As buzzed as a bee
As royal as a queen.

Olive Paterson (9)
Penketh South Community Primary School, Penketh

Friendship

F riendly

R espect

I ntelligence

E nergetic

N ice

D etermination

S portsmanship

H appiness

I ndestructible

P atience.

Ella Vaughan (9)

Penketh South Community Primary School, Penketh

Blast-Off!

Blast-off,
Blast-off,
To outer space, we go,
Two green aliens on our way home.

Blast-off,
Blast-off,
Through the deep, dark sky,
We arrive at our planet,
The Big Green Eye.

Alfie Fitzpatrick (10)
Penketh South Community Primary School, Penketh

Rugby Ball

R ough
U nstoppable
G reat
B rutal
Y outh

B rilliant
A stonishing
L ethal
L eadership.

Alfie Delamere (10)
Penketh South Community Primary School, Penketh

Family

F riendly friend
A mazing at hugs
M arvellous mum and dad
I ntelligent ideas
L ovely lights
Y ou're young and beautiful.

Sophia Prosser (9)
Penketh South Community Primary School, Penketh

Helka The Best Pony

H eartful horse
E xcellent efforts
L oving lady
K indest of kind
A mazing animal.

Lacey Pickering (9)
Penketh South Community Primary School, Penketh

What Am I?

Fire-breather
Breath-taker
Snorey sleeper
Roaring flyer.
What am I?

Answer: A dragon.

James Hemsley (9)
Penketh South Community Primary School, Penketh

Enchanted

In a glade where twilight whispers weave through
trees,
Where sunlight dances on the gentle breeze,
There lies a verse, a tapestry spun,
Of dreams and magic where all hearts run.

Beneath the boughs of ancient oaks,
Where time stands still and laughter chokes,
A brook babbles secrets, soft and clear,
Its melody calls inviting all near.

Petals of sapphire, emerald and gold,
In this enchanted realm, stories unfold,
Each flower a tale, each leaf a song,
In the heart of the forest where all belong.

The moon, a guardian, hangs low in the sky,
Casting silver beams as night draws nigh,
Stars twinkle like diamonds scattered with care,
In this wonder-filled world, magic lingers in the air.

A fae with wings of gossamer light,
Dances on dew drops, a mesmerising sight.
Her laughter, a chime, like bells in the morn
In her presence, the mundane is reborn.

The trees, they murmur, their voices entwined,
Sharing the wisdom of ages combined.
Roots deep in the earth, branches reaching high,
In this enchanted wonder, the spirit can fly.

A tapestry woven with threads of delight,
Where shadows and dreams blend softly at night,
The air is alive with the scent rare,
A fragrance of hope, of love and of care.

In this sacred space, where wonder ignites,
Imagination soars to unfathomable heights.
With every heartbeat, the magic expands,
In the enchanted wonder, where life understands.

So, come, dear traveller, let your spirit roam free,
In the heart of the enchantment, just you and me.
For within this wonder, a truth we will find,
That the heart of the universe beats in kind.

In the enchanted Wonderverse, let us dwell,
Where stories are spun, and all is well.
For in every whisper, in every glance,
Lies the magic of life, a timeless dance.

Eleanor Lloyd (10)
Red Hill CofE Primary School, Worcester

Seasons

Snow melting at the sun's fiery touch,
Elegant oaks spreading their branches wide in
welcome,
Their leaves displaying the joy of new life,
Pinks of cherry blossoms drift through the delicate
breeze,
Baby lambs prance around the newly sprouted buds of
spring,
Bees buzzing through the glimmering patches of
daffodils,
Ice melting softly, fresh grass emerging from the
ground.

The sun rises strongly in the east,
Delivering the sunshine and relaxation, the eagerly
awaiting world,
Can't wait to grasp in their greedy, impatient hands,
Indolent tourists hastily shove towels and spades into
their overflowing bags,
Violently applying enormous amounts of sunscreen,
And rushing down to the aquamarine, sparkling ocean,

Greens of leaves, slowly fade to the ambers of autumn,
Crisp leaves glide to the ground like a swallow to
stream,

Sweet smells of apple pie waft through the air,
Breaking the enchantment cast upon us all,
Animals foraging for the softest of twigs and leaves,
As the sudden spell of rest binds them for another
year.

Mabel Ferguson (10)
Red Hill CofE Primary School, Worcester

Sirens Of War

Once more the air raid siren blows
As they come again to bomb our home
As darkness falls each night we pray
That we will live to see a peaceful day

As we cower and hide beneath the earth
We see how little life is worth
In this metal bunker that protects our heads
We wish we were back in our warm beds

The sounds of thunder continue to crash
And the smell of homes turned into ash
Fills this room and fills our hearts
We huddle together, we must not part

The silence falls and daybreak has come
We climb back to Earth to see what's done
Our streets and homes lost, bombed to bits
But we must not fail, we must not quit

For tonight we will live this over again
But stronger we must become
And fight till the end

These sirens of war, these bitter sounds
As we fight for our freedom in the air and on ground
One day they will cease, this is my hope
To live without fear, bombs and guns smoke.

Andreas Mougis (11)
Red Hill CofE Primary School, Worcester

The Journey

Flowers are blossoming,
The bears are coming out to play,
They are having a picnic with all of their friends today,
The smell of roses fills the air,
Just like the smell of apple pie,
Going to a park to pick some blackberries and raspberries,
To make some crumble with your nan.

Summer is fun for everyone,
The smell of freshly cut grass,
Breathtaking sunsets as the sun goes down,
Building sandcastles,
Playing in the sea,
Having fun, you and me.

Now the leaves are changing colour,
Reds and oranges and golds,
Crunching through the leaves,
Conkers falling from their spiky shells,
Carving faces into pumpkins,
Harvest is here!

Leaves are falling off the trees,
Animals are hibernating,

They've got the right idea,
Time to turn on the fire,
Get cosy under a blanket,
Heat up the hot chocolate,
And watch some Strictly!

Emilia Myers (11)
Red Hill CofE Primary School, Worcester

Charlie's Chocolate Factory

He walks into the chocolate shop
Hoping to find a ticket,
He carefully tears the wrapper...
Charlie got the last golden ticket.

He sprints back home as quick as a flash
With the ticket in his hand,
Grandad Joe jumps out of his bed,
"I'll go with you, take my hand."

The other winners wait eagerly at the door,
For the wonder inside awaits,
Grandad Joe and Charlie
Wait eagerly behind the gates.

The golden gates swing open
And Mr Willy Wonka appears,
Past the clumps of rhododendrons,
And down by the chocolate river.

Oompa-Loompas are now in sight,
Testing out all sorts of chocolate,
Every other ticket winner has got lost or sucked up a
pipe.

Only Charlie and Grandad Joe remain,
Willy Wonka shares a little secret,
The chocolate factory is Charlie's,
This is Charlie's chocolate factory.

Orla Margetts (10)
Red Hill CofE Primary School, Worcester

Harvest

H eaps of fiery red and orange leaves drifting
   gracefully down to the damp, muddy floor

A ir is getting miserably misty and is topped with the
   beautiful smell of greasy, mouth-watering bacon

R ed evening sun is getting further away and even
   getting colder like a cup of cosy hot chocolate
   sitting out in the freezing cold

V ests are starting to be worn underneath clothes
   because the weather is getting cooler and thin
   clothes are not enough to keep us all warm

E nvironment is getting warmer because of global
   warming and icebergs are starting to melt and drift
   away from the shore

S tars are starting to go away because thick clouds
   are blocking the beautiful light out

T ractors are starting to cut the corn while slowly
   driving down the *extremely* windy country lanes,
   blocking the road so none of the other cars can get
   through.

Joseph Wickson (8)
Red Hill CofE Primary School, Worcester

Four Seasons

The newborn lambs are bleating in a luscious emerald field,
And the tender rain pattering on the pavement is teal,
I can see buttercups sprouting from the ground,
And happiness all around!

As the serene waves ripple against the creamy, lemon beach,
A ship slowly rolls out to sea which is the colour of a peach,
I lick my ice cream as I lie in the summer sun,
Everyone is having so much fun!

As the crispy, gold-tinged leaves fall,
I can hear a distant bird call,
The trees calmly sway,
In the bitter cold of day.

As the illuminated moon rises into the sky,
The final stifling rays of sun say *bye*,
I hear a piercing wolf howl,
I wonder what other nocturnal animals are on the prowl...

Alanna Lord (10)
Red Hill CofE Primary School, Worcester

The Battlefield

This war was cruel, deadly, disastrous
So many lives lost, so many lives to give.

The battlefield of no man's land and unmarked graves
Of the noble ten million horses, ten million men.

Death bringer
Heart breaker
Fear coming
Darkness looming
Apocalypse now

War is terrible
Especially this one
Death at every turn

The 6th May 1945
We won in Europe
No not again; not so soon!
It was still raging on, somewhere else
So we were called to fight and to brave fright upon
fright

Then September 2nd, 1945
We won!

There was peace
There was life

Then the poppies burst
There was peace
There was life
There was freedom
For the first time in six long, horrible years

Happily ever after?

Farhan Amin (10)
Red Hill CofE Primary School, Worcester

Keep Trying

One, two, three, four, five, I like football,
A little bit of basketball.
I like English and French.
When I am in my garage, I use a wrench.
I see the sky
I wish I could fly.
It's nearly the end
In five, four, three, two, one.
I'm only joking, I haven't said the end.
So, we're not done,
So, we're going to carry on.
School is a nice, beautiful place.
You can see on my face.
It's in my mind, and I would love to read standing up on my chair, for these words to go through my hair.
Saying this out loudly like I do.
I like to pray
Like I do all day.
I love good food, it makes me strong.
Because God will not let anything go wrong.
Keep trying, I'm not lying!

Izaan Ali (9)
Red Hill CofE Primary School, Worcester

A Magic Wonder

Wonderland is the perfect place,
To watch bunnies having a race,
To see different coloured clouds,
And see unicorns that will make you go *wow!*
Wonderland is the perfect place,
To learn that the kindness you give,
Can help others learn how to believe.

If you learn how to hope,
It will help you manage and cope,
Wonderland is part of the Wonderverse,
Inside it, you can learn how to be a pony nurse.

Wonderland will give you light,
Enough to fly a fantastic kite,
Even at night,
There are glowing flowers growing in sight.

So why not visit the Wonderverse,
I promise you won't get a curse,
So put on your magnificent shoes,
And look out for the magic clues.

Noah Keatley (10)
Red Hill CofE Primary School, Worcester

Super Pig

Slug-rhinos slither down the hills of cheese
Fish horses swim through orange juice
While the frog dogs leap.

But up in the sky
Where the gorilla birds glide
What do I see?
A *super pig.*

Saving the day
Super pig flies over the sea and through the sky
What is that? A monkey ant
About to *die.*

He crashes down onto the ground
Where he sees
A monkey ant *drowning*
He jumps into the river
But he can't swim
Who will save the day?

Will it be *Jim*?
He leaps into the river
And yes he can swim
He takes them out

And they get dry
And I'll tell you all
That was a *lie*...

Jude Hulme (10)
Red Hill CofE Primary School, Worcester

Seasons

S pring, summer, autumn, winter – these are the
seasons, all four in a year

E very year, they repeat, and as the sun sets, they
stay with us day and night

A utumn reds, winter blues, spring pinks, summer
yellows – these are the colours you might find at
the right time

S ee the frosted grass, blooming flowers, hear the
crunchy leaves and feel the bright emerald greenery

O n the early morning walks, the dawn hour chimes
and the fresh water blooms the greenery

N othing makes me happier than the morning sunrise
on my face, nice and early, never late

S o don't take these lovely things for granted
because, without these, life wouldn't be the lovely
life we have.

Hayley Cartwright (10)
Red Hill CofE Primary School, Worcester

The Animals That I Didn't See!

I didn't see a cow with a green face,
Or ride a parrot into space,
I didn't see a cheetah read a book,
Or a snake with a weird look.

I didn't see a bunny with a horn in Spain,
Or a kangaroo with a terrible pain,
I didn't see a dinosaur in a race,
Or ride a monkey into space.

I didn't see a dragon wearing glasses,
Or a pig that does break dances,
I didn't see a talking fish in the stream,
Or a unicorn flying into my dream.

I didn't let the pig let out his gasses,
Or let a lion have school classes,
I didn't see a flamingo down in the sea,
Or a popcorn in a crocodile's teeth.

Sophie Bogdan (10)
Red Hill CofE Primary School, Worcester

Harvest

H arvest is the most important festival as well as religious festivals

A utumn is the season that it is in. You step on crunchy leaves in the month of October

R ipe fruit pops out of the ground and that is what we eat

V egetables mostly grow in the ground and fruit grows on trees

E very fruit and vegetable is from the muddy ground; some are small like an ant, and some are big like an anteater. They come out satisfyingly

S unshine is not always there but that is good because we can have rain and the rain waters the fruit and vegetables

T asting tall fruits and vegetables, it's delicious.

Happy harvest!

Stella Chapman (8)
Red Hill CofE Primary School, Worcester

My Wonderverse

As I stepped forward, I saw a magical door calling my name,
I knew it wanted me,
I stepped closer, bubbles of excitement shot through my stomach,
My heart was racing fast,
This was it,
My dream come true...

There were butterflies, fairies, pixies and even talking trees,
Where was I?
I could see little fairy houses and pixie dust,
The busyness sizzling in my toes,
Long, pretty, pink bridges and light-up lanterns,
Tiny fairy houses glistening in the glow,
Dark green mossy blankets as roofs for little pixies,
I felt ticklish green grass slipping through my toes,
Like the dew on top of tents in the middle of June.

Adnae Bateman (10)
Red Hill CofE Primary School, Worcester

Religion Counts

Religion, a dove that flies
It carries stories that are real
Stories that talk about God and love
Your belief counts
You won't make a relief
You're gonna be proud
So be loud.

God created you to be amazing
So make God say, "Wow!"
By going *pow!*
And you should pray or God may go and say
Start to pray and be amazing
Just like what God was saying.

Every single day God counts
And he doesn't need to be in a pod
And always remember religion counts
Like Brussels sprouts.

It's after play so come and pray
It's your time to shine and be unique.

Archie Sandford (9)
Red Hill CofE Primary School, Worcester

The Multiverse

For those who don't believe in the multiverse,
You shall learn that it's real.
The multiverse is a world of nothing and everything at
the same time.
It has candy cane forests with white snow
Pixies deep within the candy cane forest's coat of arms.
It has paint fields where nothing,
I say nothing,
Is cooler!
It has yellow grass and pink trees.
The multiverse also has a cold lava valley.
It is not normal
But it is a place of lava that is blue and very cold.
It would give you frostbite
So it's very dangerous.
Now you should believe it.
Pray there is also a sandcastle town, a town made.

Archie Hume (10)
Red Hill CofE Primary School, Worcester

Harvest

H ard-working farmers growing crops outdoors,
sharing vegetables and fruit, and don't forget,
there's also time to give donations

A utumn is when the leaves fall in different colours
like red, brown, orange and green. The weather is
autumnal during harvest

R usty leaves, wet grass, amazing flowers and
animals

V egetables and fruit are all for the harvest to make
everybody full and happy

E verything fresh, everything clean, all to help the
homeless

S eeds and sharing, celebrations and festivals to get
ready for harvest

T he tasty vegetables and fruits are all for you and
everyone.

Jasmine Whitehead (8)
Red Hill CofE Primary School, Worcester

Cats, Cats, Cats

It was a rainy day
Like the clouds had held
Their tears in for a century
Earsplitting thunder echoed
Through the City of London,
Thinking how I long to travel
To a place called Sundom
Although if you were to travel
Into space, you would find
That the rings of Saturn
Were no longer rocky based
And had transformed into unsurprisingly
Adorable bubble-headed cats.

The television box sat on my bedside table
And the words it said really got my attention
"It's raining cats!" it spoke
I had to give myself a poke
To check I wasn't dreaming.

Luna Kellitt (10)
Red Hill CofE Primary School, Worcester

Being Happy Matters

Family, friends,
Smiling, laughing,
Looking outside, nature as beautiful as a new book,
Watching clouds dancing through the sky.

Splish, splash! Swimming down the pool to the other end,
Swoosh! Swirling around the floor, dancing all the way,
Running all day long, playing with friends, running all day,
Beautiful pictures being coloured, so many colours.

Family, friends, smiling, laughing,
Looking outside, nature as beautiful as a new book,
Baking cakes, tasty mixture, for my tummy, for my tummy,
Looking after pets all day long, always caring for everyone.

Izzy Hart (9)
Red Hill CofE Primary School, Worcester

Harvest

H oney is worth money for all the hard-working farmers for all the late hours

A utumn leaves fall. When the day's been long, we greet the hard-working farmers and shout out, "Hey!"

R ain means all the crops can grow to be as fresh as ever and we also get fresh water

V oices are humming a lovely song in the happiest of tunes

E ggplants are growing bigger and bigger, getting ready to be harvested

S haring food on Thanksgiving and being with your lovely parents and family

T he farmers take their time and care for our plants so we can be strong and healthy.

Valentina Guest (8)

Red Hill CofE Primary School, Worcester

My Emotions, My Decisions

Happiness, all smiles, all laughs, beaming, healing my sadness.
Sadness, don't deny it, you are sad, don't say "I'm not crying", trust me, soon you'll be glad.
Anger, shouting, yelling, fighting, only misunderstood, mad not glad.

Anxiety, protecting you from scary things you cannot see,
Fear, protecting you from scary things you can see,
Boredom, waiting, hating, nothing but loud silence,
Bravery, bold and daring, standing up for what's right,
Hope, not giving up, just listen up, I hope for the best!

My feelings count, just don't let the anger out.

Sadie Luck (9)
Red Hill CofE Primary School, Worcester

Counting Friendship

C ount your friends in everything you do,

O ne wrong move, everything is gone from you,

U s, together, we need help up from falling over and help in work,

N o one is lost out on the street and left out on a playground to sit there,

T o everyone that leaves you out, someone out, let them play with you,

I n everyone, soul and heart, needs to be warm, then someone will help,

N o one gets in trouble if you help them not do things they want to do,

G oing to help the homeless is a good thing to do, sort them out, help them to go to a home that gives support.

Callum Atherage (10)
Red Hill CofE Primary School, Worcester

Happiness To Me

Happiness to me is having fun with my family,
Like friends playing with my pets,
Me playing with my toys,
Or being at the beach,
All of those things make me happy.

Sunny evenings or rainbows,
Maths and comedy,
Lunchtimes at school and books from the library,
That's what makes me happy.

Pets sleeping on my lap,
As silent as can be,
They're all sleeping on me,
Recharging their batteries.

The ocean is as blue as a clear sky,
Trees as green as grass,
Roses as red as blood,
I love all of these things that make me, me.

Harvey Clark (10)
Red Hill CofE Primary School, Worcester

An Amazing School

I go to school every day
I do some work and like to play

The thing I love most is art
Because my drawings are so smart

"Oh look, I've become a poet,"
And I did not know it

Henry VIII is ancient history
Before I learnt this he was a mystery!

When I get home I like to say
All the things I did that day

School is here to help us learn
We do PE and feel the burn!

In maths, we put on our thinking hats
And practise for our SATS

At school, we write lots
The amount we write can fill up pots!

Layla Bosworth (9)
Red Hill CofE Primary School, Worcester

The Disco Ball Dance

A rocket flying through space,
With stars shining bright all around,
The solar system turning,
But suddenly it crashed on the ground.

What a mysterious planet this was,
Stardust sprinkling on his head,
It was like a magic dream,
Except he wasn't in bed.

He heard distant music,
Saw aliens coming his way,
But they were not like normal aliens,
They looked like disco balls today.

The astronaut's arms started to drop,
He was being hypnotised by the music of the best,
It went all blurry,
He was becoming an alien like the rest.

Isla Powell (10)
Red Hill CofE Primary School, Worcester

Fabulous Feather Flowers

Flowers blooming in the distance
Elegant little fairies popping out slowly
New colours being born

On the top of the fairy tree
Lived a little feather flower, little flowers
They look like feathers
Blue, red, indigo, colours of vibrant beauty

The seasons change from frosty winters
To summer-like springs
Powers grow from magic fairy dust

One early morning, it's time
The feather flower gently opens
An elegant fairy is born
Blue and purple hair, beautiful blue eyes
Purple wings with patterns of grace
A world full of wonder!

Neevie Burfitt-Delord (10)
Red Hill CofE Primary School, Worcester

Happiness Tree

Happiness to me
Is like a tree
One branch is sunshine
It's really quite divine

Another branch is family
The next one is PE
Another one is books
And I really like to cook

The next one has to be the oceans
They're like pretty potions
Nature is something I love
My favourite bird is a dove

The trunk is me
I can't forget bees
Or rainbows too
Or the picture I drew

The leaves are sweets and treats
Another branch is my football team
And don't forget ice cream
This is what makes me, me.

Annabelle Hadland (9)
Red Hill CofE Primary School, Worcester

Heroes

Heroes are standing up for what is right,
To make all of our futures bright,
And they don't have to be fictional or have powers,
Because they are heroes,
David Attenborough, Rosa Parks,
All of them,
Greta Thunberg, Issac Newton,
None of them need a power.

They warn us about the environment,
They discover the laws of physics,
They protest for what is right,
No matter if it takes them out of the spotlight,
They do what they must,
To keep Earth from turning into dust,
And the reason they do this,
Is because they care about us.

Rowan Casey (10)
Red Hill CofE Primary School, Worcester

Harvest

H arvest is when we thank people who do all the hard work and make delicious food for us

A utumn is when harvest happens. There are always beautiful displays of orange, yellow and red leaves on the ground.

R ipe food is what we expect at harvest time; there are ripe rows of vegetables

V egetables are very healthy and the vines are getting longer

E arth is very amazing and exciting, it provides food for us

S unshine is very beautiful during harvest, you can smell all the fresh vegetables

T he tasty food is the best thing about harvest.

Ruth Barton (8)
Red Hill CofE Primary School, Worcester

The Four Seasons

The chilly winter snow falling gently down,
The fire burning bright with all of its light,
The blankets are hugging you day and night.

Amongst the fields, lambs are born,
The wrappers of Easter eggs are all torn,
This time is right,
Playing day and night.

As warmth grows,
Let's put on a water show,
Licking my lips for ice cream,
We're having so much fun
Everybody, *scream!*

The autumn is here,
The cold is near,
All the leaves on the trees fall,
Red, orange, brown,
I could name them all.

Connie Middleton (11)
Red Hill CofE Primary School, Worcester

Our Magical Planet

Autumn comes, summer goes,
Crunchy leaves, family of bears
Coming... going...
Tweeting birds chirp away.

The enchanted house will always be there
With fairies dropping pixie dust all through the air.

Deers playing day by day
Running from friends...
Galloping through trees
With mythical creatures
Flying higher than bees.

Climate change is happening
Year by year...
Forest creatures are going to end in tears
Please make a change or our world will end
And tears of sadness will rise
Again!

Bonnie Bruce (10)
Red Hill CofE Primary School, Worcester

Numbers

N umbers, one... two... three... Can my friend beat me to count to one million or even a billion?

U nder the sea, there are 1,000,000,000,000 grains of sand. Every year, I earn a grand, and at the end of the year, I deserve a big cheer

M y voice is strong, there is nothing wrong

B ut it gets tired at the end of the day

E very number, every word, I count as fast as a flying bird

R oman numerals, I know they're so complicated and slow

"S on, don't be a mathematician, get a better job in life."

Magnus Price (9)
Red Hill CofE Primary School, Worcester

Space Adventure

We're on an adventure through space
We went to Mars, it was ace
We've seen Venus and Mars
We looked up at the stars
We're on an adventure through space

We're exploring the galaxy
We'll see what we will see
We'll see the Milky Way
And weird spins and twists while covered in mist
We explored the galaxy

We're seeing the universe
Or maybe the multiverse
We've seen Venus and Mars
Galaxies and stars
We've explored, we've explored, we've explored.

Jonah Dewhurst (10)
Red Hill CofE Primary School, Worcester

Do You Know...

A super riddle about superheroes!
Do you know...

Who has a surfboard but has never seen the sea?
Has no denture but complete silver teeth?
Lives in space but can always breathe?
Is completely silver but is not wearing jewellery?

Answer: Silver Surfer.

A wet riddle!
Do you know...

What has a bark but is always broke?
Has a mouth but cannot drink coke?
Can run but cannot walk?
Makes a sound but cannot talk?

Answer: A river.

Niamh Jackson (10)
Red Hill CofE Primary School, Worcester

Harvest

H andmade fruit and vegetables, ready to be shared

A nimals eating all of the aubergines on the farm

R ed combine harvesters crunching and crushing the crops

V egetables that are sweet and sour, but fruit is still better

E arth is pretty amazing during harvest, it makes all the fruits and vegetables grow

S unshine helps the crops to grow but they also need water

T asting fruits and vegetables is really fun. You get to see which ones are sour, sweet, crunchy and soft, but also spicy.

Elsie Prigg (8)
Red Hill CofE Primary School, Worcester

Together Forever

F riends are forever.

R unning together doesn't matter if I lose.

I play with my friends all day.

E ating together is what matters.

N o matter what, we will always be friends.

D on't bully anyone because everyone's unique.

S chool friends aren't the only friends, family are ones as well.

H ow do you connect with friends?

I respect everyone because everyone is different.

P lay dates are always fun no matter the differences we have.

Bella Nash (10)
Red Hill CofE Primary School, Worcester

Everyone And Everything

I love my family
I love my pets

My friends, uncle and aunt
My dog, cat and hamster
When I fall down, my friends help me
When I feel ill, my parents take me to the doctor

The nature, ocean and sand
Colour, crayon and drawing
Creatures, animals and fish
My favourite crayon and colour is blue

I like sports and games:
Cricket, tennis and football
I love going to the park on the swing
I play games like Roblox and Minecraft

I love everything and everyone.

Badar Suleman (9)
Red Hill CofE Primary School, Worcester

Everybody's Voice Counts

On one side there's this boy.
You could call him Roy.
Another side there's this girl.
With eyes like pearls.
Their voices light up the world.
Together with rights as they shine bright.

Everybody's voice counts.
Whether they glance, in darkness or night.
So the spirit sprouts with a beaming feather.
Let out your rights, and bark at your frights,
Because together is the final dart of weather.
Our might is the final key.
Why argue? When we can all play together happily?

Sebby Iordache (9)
Red Hill CofE Primary School, Worcester

Dinosaur Roar

Long ago, before you and me,
Dinosaurs roamed the Earth and stomped their feet,
They ruled the Earth like a queen,
With silver scales and bloodshot eyes.

The existence of them feared many,
They roared and played until the sun faded away,
But sadly the day came when they had to leave,
With a big *bang!* There was no more, yes,
There was no more of the dinosaur roar.

But if you're lucky, you might just find,
What's left of the crazy dinosaur roar.
Roar!

Frances Boakes (10)
Red Hill CofE Primary School, Worcester

A World Of My Dreams

Bam! I was there - "Dilys in the wing,"
That's what my mum said as my life started
Like a bell tolling *ding ding!*
Poof! I was three and we moved, weehee!
Whizz! I was five and Ada was astride
A sister that would forever be by my side
Boom! I was ten, that's when I saw her
My best friend
Zap! Eighteen, an adult already
And for me, it is only sunshine ahead
Because we truly are all stardust
A place of my dreams.

Dilys Fox (10)
Red Hill CofE Primary School, Worcester

The Environment

Over the years, animals, environments change
Like desert, jungle and forest
Some fight for dominance
Predators hunt for food that they cannot catch for food
They cannot catch because of how fast they are
Animals know to watch out for predators
The hunt
The prey
Bears fight for dominance and hunt so much
And are eating so much
A cobra lives in the loneliness of Australia
These tough birds have razor-sharp claws
At the end of each leg
Which they use to defend themselves.

Kian Hodgson (10)
Red Hill CofE Primary School, Worcester

Harvest Happiness

H arvest is so cool; it is as fun as Christmas and you eat, eat, eat!

A utumn is now here but it only comes every year

R earing farmers flee, looking after their animals

V egetables crunch between our teeth as they are as tasty as sweets

E very year, there is a fun feast with vegetables and meat

S unshine saunters over the crops as they steadily grow

T asty treats for everyone to enjoy eating, so say thank you to the farmers for the food we eat as they grow it.

Ashton Swindlehurst (8)

Red Hill CofE Primary School, Worcester

Kindness Is Always Right

Kindness brings love,
When you treat everyone right,
But kindness will be broken
If you treat everyone wrong.

But we can fix that,
If you treat everyone with love,
And be nice to each other,
And not fight and punch.

If a wasp comes up to you,
Don't try to scare it away,
It will get mad and try,
To sting you anyway.

When you're with your family
And your parents just came home,
You should help them do chores
To give them a rest.

Mylan Le (9)
Red Hill CofE Primary School, Worcester

Harvest

H ard-working farmers spend all of their time giving us barley, wheat and oats

A pple pie is my favourite thing to eat, I also like oregano

R iveting leaves of red, yellow and amber falling off the trees

V egetables growing in the amazing autumn sun, I'm hearing the harvest samba

E very day in the countryside is so special

S pectacular air, crops and composters, watch out for stinging nettles

T errific harvest for people of all shapes and sizes.

Daisy Carpenter (8)

Red Hill CofE Primary School, Worcester

Galaxy Of The Universe

Planets in orbit around the scorching sun,
Stars twinkling in the galaxy of the universe.
Spaceship levitating closer and closer to Earth,
Jupiter's as small as a Smurf.

Aliens floating in the sky,
After that they said goodbye.
The moon glows as bright as a torchlight,
And the astronauts like to explore the spaceships flying
high.

The purple-blue space colours shine in the sky,
The sounds from the aircraft you can hear from miles
away came from up high.

Jess Gunundu (10)
Red Hill CofE Primary School, Worcester

Gymnastics Counts

Bars swinging, bars playing
Doing upward and downward circles
Oh, bars, oh, bars
Chalk, bars
Three casts, max nine
Ow, bars

Floor is poor
It rhymes with nor
Doing a backbend or cartwheel
Oh, floor, oh, floor
Now the flips and the splits

Beam, balance beam
Jump then somersault over from the top
Bing, bang, pop!
Oh, beam
Oh, that old beam

Vault, run up, jump up
And off handspring
Round off and there.

Willow Rose Forrest (9)
Red Hill CofE Primary School, Worcester

Nature Is Wonderful

Soggy leaves falling from the towering brown trees,
that sway above the people that dare to enter the
Amazon jungle.
Microscopic birds, you can hardly see them.
Spotted animals called the jaguar
That can hunt for any mighty
Prey.
Ice cold, running
Water that the animals drink from.
Monkeys swinging in motion from the tangled vines up
in the air, and the apes that groom
The babies have very scruffy hair.
This peaceful place called the jungle where nature is
wonderful.

Evelyn Thompson (10)
Red Hill CofE Primary School, Worcester

Wildlife

What could live in neutral weather?
That doesn't have one fragile feather.
Has an appealing nose,
But doesn't have any toes.
Sometimes lives in crushed-up leaves,
But never tatty trees?
Who am I?

What can live in a tree for more than a week?
But doesn't have a flashing beak,
Can survive without fresh water and food,
But is never in an alarming mood.
That has a furious and mighty family,
Which is always lively?
Who am I?

Poppy Satchwell (10)
Red Hill CofE Primary School, Worcester

Harvest

H ard-working farmers
A utumn makes the leaves yellow, orange and red
and they fall down, down, down!
R ustling bushes in the strong wind
V oices in the harvest choir
E arth, the human population's planet
S mell of harvest food at the festival
T all trees with red-orange leaves that start to fall
down.

Autumn comes before winter,
After autumn, get your woolly coats on,
And prepare for the awesome winter.

Lochlan O'Loughlin (8)
Red Hill CofE Primary School, Worcester

The Completely Normal Wood

I stepped into the wood, that's when I saw it
A tiny... little... door
A door that belonged to something...
Something small
Pixie dust surrounded it
Pink, light and fluffy
Like candyfloss

Lanterns hung from sparkling leaves,
Old wooden bridges,
Connecting either side of the crystal clear streams
I couldn't help but stop
As the sun made the water gleam
The fresh wet grass tickled my toes
Flakes that fall in winter snows.

Edie Worth (11)
Red Hill CofE Primary School, Worcester

This Is A Wonderland

The calming breeze and the buzzing of bees
Dragons flapping with pride
The sheer beauty makes me stride
This is a wonderland

Jagged rocks with curly tops
Canyons and gorges, goblins' forges
This is a wonderland

Great high peaks and little mice squeaks
Green forests and orange deserts
This is a wonderland

Witches' wagons pulled by great big dragons
Fairy mansions with glossy expansions
This is a wonderland.

Elliott Usher (10)
Red Hill CofE Primary School, Worcester

The Playgound's Corner

In the playground's corner where the shadows play,
The enchanted tree watches from a distance away.

Standing tall, providing shade,
It nurtures young caterpillars on a hot summer's day.

Enriched with memories of laughter and play,
Holding back tears from when its leaves flew away.

The enchanted tree is here to stay,
Whilst the butterflies will soon be ready to fly away.

The enchanted tree watches from a distance away.

Amelia Ishaq (10)
Red Hill CofE Primary School, Worcester

All The Things I Love

Spending time with family,
All day long,
Smiles and laughter,
Look what joy this has brought.

Let's have fun with friends,
A ray of sunshine can bring so much praise,
Let's shout hooray!

Going to your favourite place,
You love and could spend all day,
Having fun until the day is done.

Having a pet is also fun,
Big or small,
Rabbits eat carrots,
Crocodiles eat meat.

What a cool beat.

Eva Bromage (9)
Red Hill CofE Primary School, Worcester

Speak Up Now

S peak up now, let your voice be heard
P eople stand up all over the world
E very voice considered
A ll voices a drum, unfiltered
K *aboom!* Goes all inequality

U ndenied, hear people respectively
P lease hear others, like a politician

N ow they will listen to you, hear your rhythm
O nly respect people who respect you
W orld harmony, not violent coups.

Jemima Bartley-Smith (9)
Red Hill CofE Primary School, Worcester

A Mythical Journey

A wander through the woods
How I stop and gaze in awe
An enchanted world I see
What am I waiting for?

I look to my right and see blossoming flowers
I look to my left and see dragons taking showers
I look ahead and see fairies dropping magical dust
To make the plants grow
And unicorns saying hello

A tumbling waterfall up ahead
And the dazzling moonlight
I make my way to the end
Oh, what a joyful night.

Charlotte Kenney (11)
Red Hill CofE Primary School, Worcester

Everyone And Everything Matters

Everyone is people,
Everything is nature.

People are friends and family,
And nature is animals and plants.

Some people like nature,
Some people like playing,
Some people love sunshine,
But some people like calm things.

I am thankful for the kindness,
And I am thankful for forgiveness,
I am thankful for calmness with nature,
And having fun with people.

Everyone and everything matters.

Ivy-May Halliday (9)
Red Hill CofE Primary School, Worcester

The Sunshine Counts To Me

I love looking at the sunshine every day
And I turn as bright as the sun
Everything I see shines out

Around the world and I just sit down and
When I look out at the sunshine
I feel like pieces of diamond shining silvery
And I feel like I am in heaven

I feel calm as I go back to school
I always go and stand next to the sunshine
I am the sun's BFF and I feel how I feel
The sunshine is as big as a moon.

Matipa Sabaya (9)
Red Hill CofE Primary School, Worcester

Sports!

Sports, sports, sports, running, rugby, rounders,
I'm swimming and I'm winning,
Cricket is bowling and batting around,
When I play rounders, I get a round,

Riding a horse is a difficult sport,
You need something for it to jump over.
How about some forts?
And as they run, they squash clovers,

Skating is fun,
As fun as eating a bun,
For a warm-up you jump,
I always like to bounce over a bump.

Joseph Cuckston (9)
Red Hill CofE Primary School, Worcester

Harvest

H arvest is important to farmers because that's when they make delicious fruit and try their hardest

A utumn's when plenty of fruits fully grow and we enjoy them

R ain helps the farmers to water the plants

V ivid leaves glowing in the beautiful sky

E ggs crack wonderfully and they help the babies

S trong farmer working very hard to help his family

T rees grow delicious and amazing fruit.

Mohammed Baruwa (8)
Red Hill CofE Primary School, Worcester

Friends

Friends, they care for you
They look out for you
And they will always love riding a bicycle
Or a tricycle
Or play tag and hide-and-seek with you

There are tons of games to play together
At home in bad weather
Or you and your friends
Can go to the park together

Your friends will help you
Care for you
Wherever you go
And wherever you are.

Your friend
Lovely, kind and gracious.

Tobias Wung Hean Ko-Newitt (9)
Red Hill CofE Primary School, Worcester

Stardust

Aah, life is lovely on the moon,
Jumping all over the place,
And who said aliens are creepy?
They are so kind...

The first few days on the moon
Have been smooth,
It's cool,
And the aliens help me find food,
So I can stay alive,
I love the moon.

But when I heard a big bang,
All the aliens went to cover,
Before I knew it,
I couldn't see any more aliens,
So I went under cover.

Thijs Molenschot (10)
Red Hill CofE Primary School, Worcester

Harvest

H ard-working farmers in all the lonely fields
A utumn days when the grass is jeweled
R ustling and crunching leaves being trampled on
V egetables all around in the fields, left and right
E very day, you go out and see dirt. It looks boring
but things we eat spring out of it
S unshine hiding behind the clouds, getting ready and
sleeping till next year
T all leafless trees are unable to grow.

Grayson Needs (8)
Red Hill CofE Primary School, Worcester

Harvest

H ard-working farmers growing and planting food, fruit and vegetables

A pples falling off the trees in the autumn

R ose-red leaves crunching and falling off the autumn trees

V egetables crunching while the chefs are chopping

E xciting time for a harvest festival

S eeds so sunflowers, flowers, fruit and vegetables can grow and we can eat

T hanksgiving dinner with your grandparents and family.

Ajwa Ayub (8)
Red Hill CofE Primary School, Worcester

My Secret Wonderland

I entered. Lively music jolted in my ears,
Shining lights dangled down, pixies glowing
But no one knowing,
Sweet fumes filling the air,
Mysterious noises in the dragon's lair,
Flowers glowing a wonderful sight,
Phoenixes fly in the starry night,
Moss cuddling the decaying log,
Unicorns pouncing hop by hop,
Candy clouds looking over the
Fireflies in the galaxy skies,
Collecting nectar like butterflies.

Scarlett Carroll (10)
Red Hill CofE Primary School, Worcester

Family

My mum, my dad and my brother
We live in a house
Altogether
We play lots of games
We sing a song
And most of the time
We get along
I have two black and white
Cats
They love to play
They come in for their food
And then run away
Then, they come back to rest
For another day
All of my family
Counts for me
And love me
And that's the poem
Of my family.

George Wiltshire (9) & Henry
Red Hill CofE Primary School, Worcester

About Me

Family, friends,
Sunshine in the blue, bright sky,
Sniffing flowers outside,
Dancing, swimming.

Playing with my teddies and toys,
Cuddling my teddies more,
Sitting down and reading a fresh new book,
Dogs and puppies bring me joy – fluffy, cute and sweet.

Making friends makes me happy,
Playing with my friends all day long,
Music makes me happy,
Music makes me dance and feel nice.

Bella Jenkins (9)
Red Hill CofE Primary School, Worcester

Your Feelings Count

Your feelings count,
Don't let your anger out,
Be on the good side,
With kindness and pride.

I know that feelings could be wrong,
I know to make them right,
I know what's right for me and you,
Just feel the feelings you feel inside.

Your feelings like to speak,
But sometimes they don't make a peep,
They know what's right and wrong,
You feel your feelings all day long.

Lucas Burt (9)
Red Hill CofE Primary School, Worcester

Space

Meteors dashing through the sky
Set on fire and blasting through all the planets
Far, far away in the galaxy
Now getting closer and closer to Earth
How long will it take?
No one knows!

The stars are getting brighter
And the sun is made of fire
The flaming hot sun is actually a star
Exploring all the different planets
Like Jupiter and Mars and don't forget...
Earth and all the stars!

Millie Burt (11)
Red Hill CofE Primary School, Worcester

About Me

Friends, family,
Laughing, smiling,
Sunshine, sport, swimming,
Watching nature, being outside as beautiful as a new
book.

Music, melody swirling around my ears,
Melody medley of music bouncing around my head,
Music medley swirling around my ears,
Music, music bouncing around my head.

Watching clouds dance in the sky,
Clouds that look like familiar faces,
Puffy, fluffy, white or grey.

Ben Prigg (9)
Red Hill CofE Primary School, Worcester

Future Nature

Walking along the bridge
That creaks so loud
That makes any head
Spin carelessly around.

From the corner of my eye
Pink sand that looks so cool
And water that glistens so much.

It makes me want to jump
Just like a kid in a pool.

Mountains so far away
But look so cool.

As I walk along the bay
The sun rises so slowly
It makes my heart beat and glow.

Charlie-James Humphries (10)
Red Hill CofE Primary School, Worcester

Don't Give Up

Believe in yourself,
Don't give up,
There's a story to tell,
Your portrait, your health,
I'm counting on you,
To change the world,
Love, kindness, happiness,
And all of the above,
We are strong, we are believers,
We are soldiers at war,
Our voice counts,
So listen out,
No one can stop us,
We believe in our voice,
I'm counting on you,
Never give up.

Molly Jane Weaver (9)
Red Hill CofE Primary School, Worcester

Harvest

H arvest is a big celebration of all our foods

A pples falling off our trees, then they're soon in our stomachs

R ed, flaxen, amber and maybe even pistachio leaves falling from trees!

V ery busy farmers making the food we eat

E very harvest is a special time for everyone

S un shines brightly, what a beautiful sight!

T aste those yummy foods - yum, yum!

Zachary Smith (9)
Red Hill CofE Primary School, Worcester

Animals Are Friends

A nimals are humans' best friends.

N ature is where we live.

I guanas, lizards, snakes and Komodo dragons are lovely animals.

M any pets are dogs, cats, or guinea pigs, but snakes are too.

A n animal supports you through anything.

L earning about different species every day.

S chool trips to zoos and class pets are still *animals*.

Phoebe Dyson-West (10)
Red Hill CofE Primary School, Worcester

Friend

F riends are fun to play sports with

R elationships with my friends might not be good one day

I would still be friends with them because they're my friends

E very friend I have will always keep me happy

N ever have my friends not cheered me up when I'm sad - they're like clowns

D oubt would never come into my team because of my friends.

Archie Ross (9)

Red Hill CofE Primary School, Worcester

Family

Family is love
Are supporting, they help
They make me feel happy
And they make me feel I am loved
They are helping me
Do things for me
And they're protective
And kind and caring
When I am poorly they help so I am not
Walk me to school and I get a little calmer
And when I go home they are kind
And nice bed
Help me feeding the cows and the sheep.

Phoebe Leighton (9)
Red Hill CofE Primary School, Worcester

Harvest

H arvest festival, it's that time of year
A utumn leaves crunching on the ground
R adishes ready to be crunched, crunched, crunched
V egetables ready to be dished up - yum, yum, yum!
E verybody loves the harvest feast to eat, eat, eat
S unshine is growing plants ready to eat, eat, eat
T ime to eat the harvest feast, feast, feast!

Jack Kimbell (8)

Red Hill CofE Primary School, Worcester

Harvest

H arvest time only comes once a year
A utumn is when apples grow on trees
R ed rustling leaves crunch as we trample on them
V egetables are yummy and as small as your tummy
E very harvest, we have fun
S un shines all over the fruit and vegetables
T asting fruit that's nice and fresh, who wouldn't
want it? It's the best!

Verity Don Gentry (8)
Red Hill CofE Primary School, Worcester

What Counts To Me

C ones and cones of ice cream - yum!
O *osh* goes the beat of the rock star's drum,
U nder the water, the shells glimmer like stars,
N *yowm!* Go the loud, speedy racing cars,
T he summer spent in the sun
I love going on a run
N ight-time always looks pretty, as do
G oals going in from Leicester City.

Teddy Thompson (9)
Red Hill CofE Primary School, Worcester

Autumn

A utumn is a wonderful time to harvest food

U nder the daylight, farmers work all day harvesting crops

T he sound of spooky Halloween is drawing near - *Wooo, wooo!*

U p above the tall trees, the owl is going *hoot, hoot!*

M onsters lurking around your garden at Halloween

N otorious farmers growing pumpkins as big as boulders.

Ella-Rose Crack (9)
Red Hill CofE Primary School, Worcester

Autumn

A mazing apple strudel made from autumnal apples

U npleasant smell of manure and doodles on the shed's wood

T he taste of apple pie and a portion of baked bacon the size of a mountain

U nforgettable season of mooing cows and giving

M innows darting down the stream

N othing will beat the kind, incredible act of giving gifts to the needy.

Alfie Cutler (9)
Red Hill CofE Primary School, Worcester

Love And Care

Friends count,
My parents' voices,
Give me a moment to write a special poem,
Or a happy song.

Sometimes I like to be supportive,
Sometimes I don't like to be sad,
I stand up for what we say,
Sometimes I make people joyful,
You can carry the sunshine and the rain,
You wear the nature,
You make people peaceful when they're joyful.

Scarlett Clark (9)
Red Hill CofE Primary School, Worcester

School Is Cool!

School is cool and it's a pool of learning,
When you're turning your brain to train,
When you learn something new, you're changing lanes,

But not in a road,
It's a code,
Where you load your brain with smart ideas,
Like engineers who design chandeliers.

When you learn, you lose all your fears,
And find out your dream careers!

Alfred Cantin (9)
Red Hill CofE Primary School, Worcester

Harvest

H arvest is a festival in autumn where we celebrate our food

A pples are falling from trees with beautiful orange leaves

R oots join to make baby trees that grow next to trees that are losing their leaves

V oices laughing in the cold

E xciting times playing conkers

S ound of crunching vegetables

T aste of apple pie.

Sam Bartlett (8)

Red Hill CofE Primary School, Worcester

Harvest

H arvest is a time in autumn

A nd people should appreciate the farmers

R adiant sunlight shines and rain pours on the farmers

V ery tasty vegetables growing in the earth

E very single farmer works very, very, very *hard!*

S unshine makes the vegetables grow

T asty, tasty vegetables growing in the earth.

Seb Whelan-Jones (8)

Red Hill CofE Primary School, Worcester

Show Your Voice

C ommunicate with others and don't be afraid to show your true self.

O ther people are different so show yourself.

U se your voice and show who you are!

N ever be afraid.

T ake your time and believe!

I magine how great it would be if your voice could shine!

N ever give up.

G o ahead and shout!

Dulcie Stayte (9)

Red Hill CofE Primary School, Worcester

About A Tiger

A kennings poem

Screeching howler
Night prowler
Grass prowler
Night seer
Day eater
Claw scratcher
Night sleeper
Large hunter
Orange starer
Predator winner
Creature hurter
Prey stalker
Claw sharpener
Brave lover
Stripy stalker
Loud growler
Fast runner
Fearless meat eater
What am I...?
I'm a tiger!

Zoya Riaz (7)
Red Hill CofE Primary School, Worcester

Speak Up

C ricket counts towards keeping me fit
O f course, not everyone plays cricket
U nderestimate me - boo! Believe in me - yeah!
N ever think you've got no one on your side
T he friends of mine
I f I'm sad they keep me as my happy self
N ever underestimate yourself
G o and project your voice!

Ellis Wade (9)
Red Hill CofE Primary School, Worcester

Tomorrow

Sometimes when I go to bed,
I think about the day ahead,
Will I be happy or will I not?
It is a mystery, is it not?
Sometimes when I go to bed,
I think about the day ahead,
Day ahead,
Day ahead,
Day ahead,
I wonder what the day will bring,
Sorrow or lots of singing,
Sometimes when I go to bed,
Bed,
Bed,
Bed.

Holly Scorer (10)
Red Hill CofE Primary School, Worcester

Harvest

H ave you heard that our food is in trouble

A nd that crops will die as temperatures double?

R ainy winters will wash away the soil

V egetables will go rotten and spoil

E veryone can help stop climate change now

S o here's what you do, I'll tell you how

T ake trains not planes and eat fewer cows.

Martha Casey (9)
Red Hill CofE Primary School, Worcester

Harvest

H arvest is when farmers grow their crops

A utumn apples grow on the trees

R ed leaves fall off the trees

V egetables are ready to be eaten - tasty, tasty

E very time a leaf falls, a vegetable is ready for us all

S carecrows working hard to save those crops

T ime is falling like the leaves on the trees.

Elliott Carroll (8)

Red Hill CofE Primary School, Worcester

Harvest

H uge, hard-working harvest!
A utumn apples everywhere,
R ed crunchy leaves that sound like crackling fire,
V egetables, nice and yummy,
E at all your fruit and vegetables,
S team coming from the factory,
T hank you for the fruit and vegetables and all the crops, animals and especially the farmers.

Alfie Majhu (8)
Red Hill CofE Primary School, Worcester

Harvest

H arvest is a celebration for our hard-working, helpful, generous farmers
A pples are as red as a rose
R eady to be picked carrots in the muddy dirt
V egetables and fruits are ready to eat
E ggs being laid and sent to stores
S eeds getting planted in the soil
T ransported to the shops to be bought.

Oscar McAree (8)
Red Hill CofE Primary School, Worcester

Imagination

Sometimes I look at the right side
Sometimes I do the right thing
Sometimes I talk about simple things
Sometimes I talk about serious things
Every time someone wins
Someone will lose
Sometimes the day will be filled with joy
Sometimes the day will be normal
Sometimes I stand like a tree
Sometimes I move like the wind.

Steev Sony (9)
Red Hill CofE Primary School, Worcester

Fruit And Vegetables

Healthy and lovely food
Helps to keep you awake and have a mindful brain
Yummy as a cake, makes you wanna swim in a
wonderful lake
Fruits and vegetables eat 5x a day
Really good to turn into a timetable star
Lime is really sour, grapes are lovely, and carrots are
rock-solid
Have you seen anyone not liking fruit and vegetables?

Hamza Ali (9)
Red Hill CofE Primary School, Worcester

Staring Fox

A kennings poem

A woodland dweller
A tail wagger
A night prowler
A prey smeller
A prey sniffer
A sneaking pouncer
A screeching jumper
A silent stepper
A determined looker
An amber eye.

I am a prowling, scowling
Fox.

I like to hunt and stalk my prey
And run around the wood all day.

Penny Ferguson (7)
Red Hill CofE Primary School, Worcester

Loving Every Day

The oceans, beaches, the sunshine all day long.
But the shouting and screaming and crying are just wrong
The sun with games that family play
Which is always a good day.

The love inside all of us is always there,
With your family and friends, it never leaves,
And be happy and loving every day and forever.

Jack Downing (9)
Red Hill CofE Primary School, Worcester

The Lost Bow

The bow, oh bow,
The pretty little bow,
Tightened well,
Making you feel well,
Putting on a show,
Making your face glow.

I'm lost, I'm lost,
I have been put into the dust,
Soon I will turn into rust.
I hear the firing,
Soon I will be found,
Then I will be put down.

Elouise Murphy (10)
Red Hill CofE Primary School, Worcester

Harvest

H ard-working farmers work all day
A pples ripen in the sun and rain
R ed tomatoes, sweet and juicy, yum, yum!
V egetables ripen in the sun on a hot summer day
E very morning, leaves fall
S mooth brown conkers lie under the tree
T he big trees glimmer under the sun.

Isaac Ali (9)
Red Hill CofE Primary School, Worcester

Animals

A nimals, some are extinct and some are endangered
N ever alone, always together
I n the winter huddle together
M iddle of summer jump for joy
A nd in the autumn hunting for food
L ove animals big and small, fierce and kind
S inging birds leaping from tree to tree.

Darcey Ball (9)
Red Hill CofE Primary School, Worcester

Vegetables

V egetables are healthy

E ggs are yummy

G reen grass with mud

E ggs need cooking

T omatoes are juicy

A pples are crunchy

B ananas are yum, yum, yum!

L ettuces are crunchy

E ggs have yellow yolks

S ee the leaves falling in the sky.

Isabelle Ford (8)
Red Hill CofE Primary School, Worcester

Happiness Counts

Everyone and everything deserves happiness,
All day long, in the sunshine or the cold.
Laughing, smiling, all the time jumping,
Playing all our life.

You're happy, you're joyful,
Don't let people make you frown.
Friends and family are there for you,
Even if you're sad.

Nancy Mills (9)
Red Hill CofE Primary School, Worcester

Harvest

H arvest is a celebration of all the fruit and vegetables

A utumn leaves are crunchy and colourful

R ed and orange, the leaves turn

V egetables to have for dinner

E arth is where we live

S unshine goes and it becomes dark

T he festival is fun at harvest time.

Zeke Hodgson (8)
Red Hill CofE Primary School, Worcester

Sports

Sports, sports, sports, when you're on the court,
Rugby, rounders, running, riding,
When you're riding, you're just gliding,
When you're playing rugby, you're just jumpy.

Sports are just a thought that becomes reality,
Football and basketball can be enjoyed,
By everyone.

Josie Hawkesford (9)
Red Hill CofE Primary School, Worcester

Harvest

H arvest is a celebration of food
A utumn leaves are crunchy on the ground
R ed fruit and vegetables ripening
V egetables are tasty and healthy
E arth is giving us delicious foods
S un shining all through the morning
T he farmers are harvesting their crops.

Erick Novo (9)
Red Hill CofE Primary School, Worcester

Harvest

H arvest is a celebration of all of our delicious foods
A pples are falling from the trees
R ed fruits are delicious
V ibrant colours of the rainbow
E agerly growing food to keep us healthy
S un is shining in the morning
T ime to celebrate the harvest.

Corey Green (9)
Red Hill CofE Primary School, Worcester

Your Voice Counts

Your voice counts
So let your heart pounce
March with your feet
As we tap to the beat
Stand up for what's right
And don't give up the fight
You and I are the same
So let's not fight in vain
As we make a choice.

We stand here together
As strong as ever.

Connie Warnett (9)
Red Hill CofE Primary School, Worcester

Love Counts

You will find love,
It will turn into a dove,
It will be filled with happiness and joy,
And it will be your golden toy.

There's a bundle of love,
And it lives up above.

You can get love big or small,
After all, they're all very cool.

I love poems.

Alanna Taylor (9)
Red Hill CofE Primary School, Worcester

Autumn

A utumn leaves are crunching beneath our feet
U npleasant smell of manure from the vegetable patch
T he comforting taste of apple pie
U nforgettable time of giving and caring
M innows darting down the trickling stream
N obody will forget the harvest.

Scarlett Kidd (9)
Red Hill CofE Primary School, Worcester

Everyone Counts

Let everyone count even if they shout
Or whatever comes out their mouth,
Everyone needs a helping hand and everyone's voice
does count
No matter what differences, persevere in everything
Help other people do a good deed, that's what
Everyone needs, maybe plant some trees.

Lucas Sudabby (9)
Red Hill CofE Primary School, Worcester

Harvest

H arvest is a celebration of food
A utumn leaves falling on the ground
R ed fruit ripening
V egetables selling in stores rapidly
E arth is where we live
S unshine is healthy for our plants
T he vegetables we eat are super healthy.

Arvin Jahani (8)
Red Hill CofE Primary School, Worcester

Pets

Cats, kittens, dogs and hamsters
Welcome to my pet world
You have seen some pets already
So now I'll tell you more
Guinea pigs, rabbits and bunnies
So you've already seen the cute and fluffy
Now the weird and unusual
Snake, monkey, piranha and the end!

Sidney Thorpe (9)
Red Hill CofE Primary School, Worcester

Harvest

H arvest time's so colourful
A t harvest, so many leaves fall off trees
R ed, orange and brown leaves come
V egetables and fruits grow
E verything is amazing
S ometimes people pick up conkers
T asty food everyone eats.

Mitch Ballinger (9)
Red Hill CofE Primary School, Worcester

Harvest

H arvest, harvest, fresh food
A pples, carrots, pumpkins
R ed roses
V egetables are fresh, fruit as well
E very year, the farmers harvest
S unshine hides away; get ready for the cold weather
T asty bread and food cooking.

Skye Waldron (8)
Red Hill CofE Primary School, Worcester

Playful Puppies

A kennings poem

Bustling bouncer
Energetic sprinter
Loving looker
Furry snuggler
Eye contacter
Adorable player
Blunt scratcher
Water slurper
Fluffy shedder
Rolling runner
Snorting sniffer
Whining woofer
Yapping howler

I am a puppy!

Layla Al-Najjar (7)
Red Hill CofE Primary School, Worcester

Hunting Owl

A kennings poem

A neck turner
A fur ruffler
A beak breaker
A night hunter
An eye flier
A talon sharpener
A meat demolisher
A mouse ripper
A high flier
A land hater
A dark spooker
A gleeful camouflager

What am I?
I am an owl!

Aaryan Mitchell-Baig (7)
Red Hill CofE Primary School, Worcester

What A Brilliant World!

A kennings poem

Food hunter
Fast runner
Night eater
Food fighter
Soft runner
Happy hunter
Meat eater
Scary hunter
Sneaky spier
Meat stealer
Eye starer
Bone destroyer
Quick crusher

Put them together...
I'm a tiger!

Ethan Hart (7)
Red Hill CofE Primary School, Worcester

Feathery Fool

A kennings poem

Light sleeper
Great swooper
Angry flier
Swooping seer
Colossal flier
Orange starer
Furious stalker
Feathery flier
Fierce predator
Night seer
Fish eater
Loud screecher.

I am an owl
In a tree at night.

Hywel Brown (7)
Red Hill CofE Primary School, Worcester

Dog

A kennings poem

Food fighter
Warm heater
Excited licker
Angry howler
Ball chaser
Mud digger
Toy chewer
Bone muncher
Rude biter
Smooth stroker
Rough wrestler
Hungry hunter
Tail waggler

What am I?
I'm a dog.

Tiwatope Olabamiyo (7)
Red Hill CofE Primary School, Worcester

Seasons

Seasons
Fuchsia flowers
Luscious green leaves
Cracking brown conkers
Shivering, bare, numb oak tree
Seasons
Frosted leaves coated in blankets
Acorns hatching from shells
Piercing warm sun
Blossoming beautifully
Seasons.

Isla Smith (10)
Red Hill CofE Primary School, Worcester

The Seasons

Winter
What causes everybody to be late in winter?
What makes everybody slip
And have a lot of accidents?
What is it?

Summer
What is something kids love in summer?
Always used but never drank.
What is it?

Joshua Evans (10)
Red Hill CofE Primary School, Worcester

Puppy

A kennings poem

Crazy chewer
Play fighter
Bed maker
Loud woofer
Food fighter
Walking lover
Playful fetcher
Parent fighter
Trouble maker
Easy startler
Adventure starter
Lap warmer
Mess maker
Ball chaser
Bone chewer.

Astrid Bantock-Minton (7)

Red Hill CofE Primary School, Worcester

Lazy Puppy

A kennings poem

Bone chewer
Mud digger
Puddle jumper
Lap warmer
Food lover
Toy chewer
Ball chaser
Lead walker
Tail wagger
Claw sharpener
Sleepy snorer
Head twister
Sleepy chewer
Food demolisher
Furniture breaker.

Eva Arun (7)
Red Hill CofE Primary School, Worcester

Puppy Life

A kennings poem

Mess maker
Bone cruncher
Cat chaser
Great barker
Tail wagger
Noise maker
Walk lover
Treat lover
Cute noiser
Lap warmer
Mud digger
Puddle jumper
Winner walker
Excited chaser
I'm a puppy.

Evyn Schimmel (7)
Red Hill CofE Primary School, Worcester

Autumn Is Here

Pumpkins are orange,
Pumpkins everywhere,
Harvest time is everywhere,
Just look around and you'll see,
Be surprised at what you see,
Apples, oranges are nice,
Bananas are ripening,
Autumn is here now,
So enjoy it.

Ugochukwu David Anikwe (8)
Red Hill CofE Primary School, Worcester

I Am A Fox

A kennings poem

Garden sneaker
Meat eater
Adventurous hunter
Food demolisher
Field grazer
Bone lover
All night screecher
Prey fighter
Eye catcher
Loud sleeper
Master pouncer

Put them together
I am a fox!

Eleanor Foster (7)
Red Hill CofE Primary School, Worcester

Fox

A kennings poem

Animal catcher
Cute runner
Adventure starter
Play fighter
Night hunter
Den builder
Mess maker
Big winner
Baby carrier
Scratch lover
Forest explorer
Meat eater
Trouble maker
Loud screecher.

Susie Ross (8)
Red Hill CofE Primary School, Worcester

Loving Looker

A kennings poem

Adorable snuggler
Enthusiastic walker
Soft sleeper
Swift runner
Sneaky sniffer
Treat cruncher
Glimmering starer
Face licker
Deafening barker
Surprising pouncer
Cute yapper
It's a little puppy!

Daniel Potter (7)
Red Hill CofE Primary School, Worcester

Tree Liver

A kennings poem

Eye starer
Mouse hunter
Strong flyer
Fast swooper
Night flapper
Worm eater
Nocturnal sleeper
Nest maker
Graceful percher
Squirrel eater
Snail eater.

Put them together
I am an owl.

Phoebe Hughes (7)
Red Hill CofE Primary School, Worcester

Seasons

The pink
Flowers on the
Grand oak tree
The flowers filled
With love.

The green
Luscious trees
And as the
Leaves fall
Like feathers
And help
The water
Flow like
Butter.

Charlie Beddows (10)
Red Hill CofE Primary School, Worcester

Puppy

A kennings poem

Toy lover
Lap warmer
Food whiner
Food lover
Bone chewer
Trouble maker
Nap lover
Human licker
Ball chaser
Tail wagger
Everything chewer
Play lover
Mess maker
Doghouse liver.

Marley Joy Price (7)
Red Hill CofE Primary School, Worcester

Pumpkin

P umpkins are orange
U nderneath the soil
M onsters at Halloween
P umpkins are everywhere
K ids go trick or treating
I t looks amazing
N ever get tricked.

Jayden Gardner (9)
Red Hill CofE Primary School, Worcester

Sly Hunter

A kennings poem

Sly hunter
Champion zoomer
Speeding racer
Olympian runner
Fearless sprinter
Meat growler
Clever mover
Sneaky predator
Creature stalker
Night-vision owner.

It is a fox.

Sam Hadland (7)
Red Hill CofE Primary School, Worcester

Fox

A kennings poem

A trouble maker
A fast runner
A night beginner
An adventure starter
A meat catcher
A play fighter
A baby carer
A loud woofer
A good eater
A bed maker
A forest lover.

Myla Holliday (7)
Red Hill CofE Primary School, Worcester

The Puppy

A kennings poem

A meat lover
A cute pouncer
A fun player
A food fighter
A snack stealer
A ball player
A big cuddler
A lap warmer
A cat chaser
A big scratcher

I am a puppy.

Atousa Naderasli (7)
Red Hill CofE Primary School, Worcester

Tiger

A kennings poem

Bone crusher
Cave liver
Prey spyer
Peacock eater
Meat fighter
Tiger wrestler
Fear winner
Prey eater
Deer catcher
Tree scratcher
Prey slasher
Tiger fighter.

Edward Hill (7)
Red Hill CofE Primary School, Worcester

Rabbit Eater

A kennings poem

Claw sharpener
Fast runner
Eye starer
Rabbit hunter
Grass prowler
Predator winner
Yellow looker
Sharp biter
Large stalker
Night seer

It's a tiger.

Inaaya Shazad (7)
Red Hill CofE Primary School, Worcester

My Past

M y voice counts
Y ours too.

P ersevered through challenges
A t the hardest moments in time
S o don't forget you count
T o everyone.

Sam Heydon-Boland (9)
Red Hill CofE Primary School, Worcester

An Owl

A kennings poem

Claw sharpener
Shadow hunter
Night glider
Brave flier
Fearless predator
Excellent swooper
Loud screecher

Put them together and what have you got?
An owl!

Rayna Samuel (8)
Red Hill CofE Primary School, Worcester

Fierce Predator

A kennings poem

Predator prowler
Fierce hider
Rubbish eater
Night hunter
Dark seer
Day lier
Silent mover
Grizzly grunter
Fearless growler
Orange looking

Fox.

Carys Smith (7)
Red Hill CofE Primary School, Worcester

Tiger

A kennings poem

A hyper runner
An aggressive hunter
A fierce runner
A fierce growler
A fast sprinter
A hyper stalker
A fearless runner
An active jumper
I am a tiger.

Lucas Ko (7)
Red Hill CofE Primary School, Worcester

Puppy

A kennings poem

Ball fetcher
Mess maker
Bed maker
Sleep lover
Food lover
Loud woofer
Toy chewer
Slipper chewer
Bed chewer
Cuddle lover
Night sleeper.

Lottie Bridges (7)
Red Hill CofE Primary School, Worcester

Fearless Killer

A kennings poem

The rabbit hunter
An eye starer
A sacred hunter
A meat eater
A fish gobbler
Sharp claws
Loud roarer
Cat hunter
Lion fighter
Night vision.

Robin Purslow-Field (7)
Red Hill CofE Primary School, Worcester

Red Fox Rise

A kennings poem

Night hunter
Bone cruncher
Fur sticker upper
Grass prowler
Hearing hero
Eye starer
Grass eater
Night stalker
Night attacker
Day sleeper.

Phoebe Taylor-Dainles (7)
Red Hill CofE Primary School, Worcester

Dog

A kennings poem

Walk lover
Lap warmer
Food lover
Claw sharpener
Tail wagger
Excited licker
Ball chaser
Everything chaser
Food demolisher
Bark winner.

Zachary Mullett (7)
Red Hill CofE Primary School, Worcester

Animals

A sloth is the cutest thing ever in the world
They eat sweetcorn and they can swim for miles
Golden their colour is
They dig in the wood
They are very calm.

Gracie Green (10)
Red Hill CofE Primary School, Worcester

Space

Haiku Poetry

Meteors crashing,
Stars glistening down on Earth,
Planets orbiting.

Sunbeam ray shining,
Moonbeam covering the trees,
Darker than the night.

Alfie Don-Gentry (10)
Red Hill CofE Primary School, Worcester

Cow

A kennings poem

Mighty mooer
Tail swisher
Milk maker
Hay muncher
Grass eater
White walker
Food chomper
Fly swotter
Corn crusher
Hoof stomper.

Savio Sony (7)
Red Hill CofE Primary School, Worcester

A Dog!

A kennings poem

Graceful runner
Dramatic barker
Furious eater
Eye starer
Night seer
Fearful
Cat scarer
Good sniffer
Noisy barker
I am a dog!

Leticia Ngen (7)
Red Hill CofE Primary School, Worcester

Tiger

A kennings poem

Bone crusher
Cave filler
Eye starer
Claw sharpener
Predator winner
Tree scratcher
Tall grass hider
Food fighter
Meat demolisher.

Carter-Jorge Hodgson (7)
Red Hill CofE Primary School, Worcester

A Space Haiku

Shining stars twinkle
Rockets shooting in the sky
Planets spin around.

Ledley Gray (10)
Red Hill CofE Primary School, Worcester

Puppy

A kennings poem

Bone chewer
Ball fetcher
Sleep lover
Toy lover
Teddy chewer
Cuddle lover
Loud woofer
Nose wetter
Walk lover
Bed maker.

Grace Bates (7)
Red Hill CofE Primary School, Worcester

Fox

A kennings poem

Master sneaker
Everything chewer
Sweet nose
Cute eyes
Autumn camouflage
Food demolisher
Night out
Test taster
Earth makers.

Ariella Barnes-Bennetts (7)
Red Hill CofE Primary School, Worcester

The Guess

A kennings poem

Cute runner
Black eye starer
Wet nose camouflager
Flappy fast runner
Funny jumper
Fun swimmer
Active smuggler

I am a dog.

Olivia Hill (7)
Red Hill CofE Primary School, Worcester

Claw Catcher

A kennings poem

Prey stalker
Fearless killer
Shadow creeper
Fear hunter
Meat eater
Rapid runner
Fierce growler
Claw catcher
Loud roarer.

Rupert Luck (7)
Red Hill CofE Primary School, Worcester

Harvest

H appy

A utumn day

R oast potatoes

V egetables

E asy peasy

S amba song

T asty spaghetti.

Owen Mogford (9)

Red Hill CofE Primary School, Worcester

Foxes

A kennings poem

Day sleeper
Night keeper
Bin stalker
Far seer
Loving looker
Secret sneaker
Sly sleeper
Kind keeper
Adventurous runner.

Lyra Lewis (8)
Red Hill CofE Primary School, Worcester

Can You Guess What I Am?

A kennings poem

Day sleeper
Mice hunter
Nest maker
Night flyer
Claw scratcher
Eye starer
Loud tu-whit tu-whooer
I'm an owl!

Lyria Bateman (7)

Red Hill CofE Primary School, Worcester

Golf

A kennings poem

Tee trembling,
Club swinging,
Obstacles moving,
Ball flying,
Carefully putting,
Buggies rolling,
Thrill seeking.

Ben Nash (10)
Red Hill CofE Primary School, Worcester

Baby Fox

A kennings poem

Meat eater
Small nose
Eye starer
Food sniffer
Scratching howler
Mouse hunter
Shy runner
Den builder.

Casper Kellitt (8)

Red Hill CofE Primary School, Worcester

What Counts

What counts, looking after my friends
What counts, working hard
What counts, playing outside
What counts, having fun!

Jack Lloyd (9)
Red Hill CofE Primary School, Worcester

The Fox

A kennings poem

A fast runner
A protective hunter
A fearless fighter
A powerful beast
A prey killer
A night eater.

Lennox M (7)
Red Hill CofE Primary School, Worcester

Night Seer

A kennings poem

Fast runner
Cheeky runner
Orangey starer
Eye starer
Meat eater

It is a fox.

Chloe Margetts (7)
Red Hill CofE Primary School, Worcester

Dog

A kennings poem

Fuzzy lover
Small runner
Playful sniffer
Soft snuggler
Adorable cuddler.

Urwa Ayub (7)
Red Hill CofE Primary School, Worcester

Tiger

Loud growler
Claw scratcher
Humongous eater
Fast runner
People eater.

Leo Macdonald (8)
Red Hill CofE Primary School, Worcester

Puppy

A kennings poem

Adorable lover
Night seeker
Eye starer
Flappy ears
Energetic tickler.

Charlotte Field (7)
Red Hill CofE Primary School, Worcester

An Animal Kennings Poem

Eye starer
Tail wagger
Baby lover
Meat eater.

Louise Summers (7)
Red Hill CofE Primary School, Worcester

YOUNG WRITERS INFORMATION

We hope you have enjoyed reading this book – and
that you will continue to in the coming years.

If you're the parent or family member of an
enthusiastic poet or story writer, do visit our website
www.youngwriters.co.uk/subscribe and sign up to
receive news, competitions, writing challenges
and tips, activities and much, much more!
There's lots to keep budding writers motivated!

If you would like to order further copies of this book,
or any of our other titles, then please give us a
call or order via your online account.

Young Writers
Remus House
Coltsfoot Drive
Peterborough
PE2 9BF
(01733) 890066
info@youngwriters.co.uk

Join in the conversation!
Tips, news, giveaways and much more!

 YoungWritersUK    YoungWritersCW

 youngwriterscw    youngwriterscw